SUE HERBINE

IN SEARCH OF NEW HOPE

XULON PRESS

Xulon Press
2301 Lucien Way #415
Maitland, FL 32751
407.339.4217
www.xulonpress.com

© 2022 by Sue Herbine

All rights reserved solely by the author. The author guarantees all contents are original and do not infringe upon the legal rights of any other person or work. No part of this book may be reproduced in any form without the permission of the author.

Due to the changing nature of the Internet, if there are any web addresses, links, or URLs included in this manuscript, these may have been altered and may no longer be accessible. The views and opinions shared in this book belong solely to the author and do not necessarily reflect those of the publisher. The publisher therefore disclaims responsibility for the views or opinions expressed within the work.

Paperback ISBN-13: 978-1-6628-6222-9
Ebook ISBN-13: 978-1-6628-6223-6

DEDICATION

DEDICATED TO MY friend Amy Freeland who in my youth in Pennsylvania was my buddy conspiring with me for many adventures. We were the Queens of entertainment for the Faith Community Church College and Career group. Remember hosting the murder mystery! She also was the first to read my works of writing and encouraged me to publish them. She is the template for Starr Davis, and I hope she enjoys her exploits. (Wait till books two and three) Thanks for the support, and enjoy the book.

I am also dedicating to my friend Wendy Newell who I met later in life and too late to be a character in this book. Wendy is the wife of my former boss at Compassion International, Al, who was the best boss ever and how Wendy and I met. Wendy is my vacation buddy, and we have traveled to many places and had many adventures. She, too, has encouraged me to have this work published from the first time she read it so long ago. So Wendy, here it is. Enjoy. And, maybe you will show up in book two or three. One can only hope.

CHARACTER INFORMATION

THIS BOOK WAS actually started about thirty-seven years ago. (which explains some of the dated references) The characters in this book have become my friends over the years, and I have enjoyed bringing them to life in this book and the other two I have written, coming soon. I have been influenced by many great authors who have directed my writing style because I am a great reader. But the best influence of this book is my life. I have had a wonderfully whole life, and God has blessed me with lots of friends and experiences. Going on short-term missions has been the most significant influencer of this book, as I saw firsthand how people could live without technology. Yes, when I describe the primitive sawmill, it is because I saw one in Honduras and have a picture of it.

That being said, the characters in my book are genuinely fictional; however, they sometimes have a basis in the reality of my friends and acquaintances. Sometimes the name is the same letter for letter, and sometimes it is a bit of a stretch, but I know. If you read this book and think you are a character, ask me; it might just be you. However, if you think you find yourself and don't like what your character is doing, remember I have to let the character move with the book, not with who you are as a friend. Remember, if you are in this book, it is because I highly honor you, and it is the greatest honor I could give a friend.

PROLOGUE

It is all history now, but as history repeats itself, maybe it's worth recording. But who will there be to read this? I don't know. My name is unimportant, and I'm sure there are more like me, but I'm not sure. It started nine no ten years before the new calendar. It was so insidious that it is hard to tell precisely when it began. The networks announced a new way to rate television shows that were foolproof. Instead of being paid to have a recorder attached to your television set, now the viewer had to pay for this new device to record preferences. At first, it was expensive, allowing only the wealthy elite to participate, but soon the public outrage produced a cheaper model that looked no different. Some believed the original high price was simply a ploy to entice all to buy. In retrospect, maybe so.

Soon every interest group, religious group, or political group encouraged its members to participate to ensure their voice was heard. Some self-appointed prophets of doom proclaimed the device was a machine of the devil. No one listened, although we should have. Next, television salesmen were giving the device away with the purchase of a new television. Television sales rose immediately. People who never watched television before were now glued to their sets thinking now they could control the network. The commercials for sitcoms and dramas no longer tried to vie for your attention by a preview of the next show but by showing clips from the last show with the number of people who watched nationwide.

It became a status symbol to have watched the show with the highest rating. Instead of baby pools or football pools at work, the enterprising now had ratings pools. Other networks in neighboring nations bought the patent and duplicated the process based on the nationwide success. The system then crossed the ocean, and within five years of the first commercial, the whole electronic world was using the system. Of course, there were a few pockets of humanity who did not use the system, but with only one or two exceptions, they lived so remotely it did not matter.

Phase II was just as insidious. The system purportedly worked on the principle that a hidden camera in the television recorded who in the family watched what program. No buttons to be pressed, no effort on the part of the viewer to record his viewing pleasure, no diary to keep, just watch television. What was unknown to the general populace was that the camera also broadcasted a hypnotic beam instructing the viewer into total obedience. Testing this principle was done using a small segment of the population: the late-night watcher. At precisely 1:00 AM, a hypnotic message went out to send a post card to the network with your name and address and the words "I heard". The computer recorded precisely who was watching, and a post-hypnotic suggestion not to mention this to anyone was given. Within three days, all but ten of the thirty thousand watchers had responded. The network sent teams out to investigate those ten. Two were illiterate, two were utterly insane, and six had died of natural or catastrophic causes the next day. The device was successful, and the corporate heads held a private celebration.

The next step was to daily every hour broadcast the hypnotic request to watch the six o'clock news. Everyone watched the news within a week, but no one could have told you why each person felt the strong need to watch. At first, the mind-controlling instructions were benevolent and peaceful. People were counseled to live peacefully with their neighbors and support the local government. Elections were soon held, and when the ballots were counted, handpicked, easily controlled minds were in high government positions. These same events occurred worldwide, and within two years, all world governments were really in the control of a few network presidents.

But power, especially absolute power, breeds corruption. Certain people were not happy ruling in secret, but as they tried to become public, they suddenly died. Those still in power decided to solve the world's problems in a deadly manner. Segments of humanity felt to be non-essential to a perfect society were unexplainably committing suicide. At first, people did not take notice. A few hardened criminals scattered over the globe did not cause grief over their passing. Neither did the prostitutes or those on welfare. Eventually, though, a pattern was noticed and reported: CAUSE UNKNOWN. People did not worry yet. After all, none of these people were helpful to society.

Soon though, the next target group was a minority group. The suicides were still unexplainable, but then a new pattern was noticed. A minority living in one geographic area was, in reality, a majority living elsewhere. While no one could explain why, if a minority moved into a segregated area, the suicides stopped. It had been an unforeseen side effect, but people were now mass migrating back to native roots. Fear of suicidal insanity, as the psychiatrists called it, was the cause of this voluntary global segregation. The presidents felt all was as it should be and broadcast messages of peace and security. The world relaxed. There was no more crime or war. Atomic bombs were dismantled. Humanity breathed a sigh of relief. Each network president was given charge of their ethnic area, and the world was at peace.

Peace is elusive, though; one day, a president in charge of his ethnic group decided his group deserved world supremacy. The subliminal message that went out for the next three months was one of supremacy and dominance for us and inferiority for them. Armies were no longer needed, but soon this continent was building one covertly. The first military move was a complete massacre; two-thirds of an entire ethnic group was wiped out and became slaves to the winner.

The other presidents quickly worked on conditioning their people to fight, but it took time, and the conquering giant was progressing too fast. The total world war that broke out was one of hand-to-hand combat, stealth, ambush, and, if a broadcasting station was taken over by the enemy: mass suicide. Eventually, the truth of our deception was made known, and humanity did not just remove the device but smashed all television sets and computers. The network presidents were tried and convicted and imprisoned in one isolated prison. Over time, they killed each other off, and the survivor killed himself.

Irreparable damage had been done, though. No one trusted even their neighbor and barely their own family. Despite the well-published details of the trial and public dismantling of the system, "Big Brother" paranoia was widespread. No one had thought on their own for almost five years. World governments collapsed, and technology was lost due to fear. The war had decimated the population. Fear of being controlled by anyone caused people to move out of the cities and into the countryside to set up small two to three-family communities. Visitors were welcomed as long as they passed through quickly, as the residents protected themselves from their own shadows. Intercommunication between communities and continents had broken down entirely on all levels due to distrust of the person and the technology needed to reach the person. All around the world, airports and shipping lanes were destroyed. Each pocket of humanity isolated itself and started living a simple life.

As no one was traveling beyond their communities' cars were abandoned and left to rust. Cities were ghost towns. People became self-sufficient, living off the land and raiding from the cities what they may need for hard goods. Survivalists were right at home and would give out advise for a price. They were the mercenaries of this new world. A new calendar was started with the year 1 AT (after television), and people became readers of books. Selective books with no mention of science but mass quantities of books. The enterprising who were always around would pilfer the city libraries and trade their wares along the road and in the villages. Barter and trade were the day's currency, as, without government, money meant nothing. And so, civilization, as it had once been known, was ended. Not with a radioactive inferno with mutants left behind as had been predicted or by the complete dominance of one world government but by a self-imposed return to life as it had been in feudal times.

You, the reader of this missive, sometime in the future, may ask who I am. The single answer is a member of modern society as it was who did not watch television. I had owned a set, but as it was used so rarely, I never purchased the device, not caring what the networks put on as I usually only watched public television. Just before the network's final takeover of our minds, those on record with no device were sent one free of charge as a courtesy. I never got around to installing mine, the best mistake of my life. The only difference I noted in my friends, neighbors, and co-workers was an unreasonable need to watch the six o'clock news. Once in a while, I would catch the news at a friend's house, but since the instructions were only given for twenty-four hours, my conditioning would disappear when I turned to the news at home the next night.

Just before the war broke out, a small group of us had formed, not knowing why we were together, but we were all free from six o'clock to six thirty pm, and no one else was. As we met night after night, we discovered a common denominator, we either did not own or did not watch television. When news of the war broke out, we decided to investigate. In our city, there was only a handful of us, twenty-two in all, but we represented a cross-section of professions and expertise. Everyone used computer terminals scattered across the city, so the information gathered could not be linked to us. An electronics wizard dismantled my device as I was the only one with one. Mine was not used through neglect. They had trashed theirs with scorn when it arrived. Our genius discovered its actual use, and we found out the networks knew about us. My television was dismantled to test the theory, and a brand-new device was found newly installed. Each member of our group found the same thing. Apparently, our lack of input into the device registered concern to the networks. We quickly started turning on our sets to the news with a full-size replica sitting in front of the television. We knew the device did not pick up life signs, just a visual characteristic match.

Working now at a fever pitch, a base of operations was developed underground with a fully independent computer system that was tap-proof. A broadcasting studio was built in the hopes of counteracting the hypnotic commands, but the proper frequency could not be found. Unable to reverse the damage, we broadcast our story on public television at eight PM. The networks were unprepared for it, and enough people watched to start the television smashing that is now history. The round-up and trial happened quickly and were accomplished by other agencies, although we did contribute evidence. The war died down fast as the no longer artificially motivated stopped fighting.

The investigative branch of my group combed the corporate headquarters for more evidence for the trial and discovered a fascinating document: **Names and addresses of all persons not watching the 6 o'clock news and suspected of being subversive towards the Network.** We kept this document for future reference. Of course, everyone in our group was on the list with a few others in the city. They quickly joined our group, but because of the rapid destruction in communication, we could only make our presence known to local towns. Society was rapidly becoming suspicious of everyone and everything, so we continued fortifying our underground facility and stockpiling all information available on our computers. As the sociologist in our group realized that humanity was quickly reverting to a feudal system, we built a castle-like edifice over our underground facility.

We hid all technology from curious eyes powering everything through solar panels in the turrets and a hidden generator in the nearby waterfall. We took on the appearance of a religious Order dedicated to the healing arts and education, publicly denouncing science and technology. Our now extensive underground labyrinth was not only deep but capable of holding most of society's modern prototypes. In addition to the castle, we had cottages for the families of our Order, and in the castle, there was a dormitory for the students at the school and the wards for the hospital. Over the years, we built up a solid reputation so that scattered communities bought their sick to us to heal and they're young to educate. We were idealists and felt we had humanity's future in our hands, but it was a precarious balance.

The year is 7 AT, but the general population has forgotten what the T stands for. Humanity is eking out an existence but becoming more isolated each year. People appear ignorant of the events leading up to our present situation. Our phycologist explained it as a mass hysterical mental block. It may also be self-preservation. From the years 1-3 AT, anyone mentioning science, technology, or television was stoned to death without a trial by an angry mob. A favorite curse used by an irate merchant who feels cheated is "May the television eat out your mind." But like most profanity, its source is forgotten. The isolated two to three-family dwellings have grown to clusters called villages, usually surrounding a large walled edifice known as the protectorate. We named ours the New Hope.

BOOK I

CHAPTER 1

FROM THE TOP of the rise, he could just make out the top of the waterfall. After four and a half years of searching, he hoped it was finally the waterfall he sought. He was average in height with light brown hair that, for him, was exceptionally long, reaching to the shoulder. His beard also could use some tending but then, it had been a long trip, one he hoped would end soon. He dismounted his chestnut-colored steed and gave Gregory a bit of carrot. He swore that sometimes the horse knew what he was thinking and was as nervous in an excited sort of way as he was.

"Steady there, boy, relax. We have been through too much these last five years together. Don't bolt on me now."

Of course, that would never happen. Gregory did not even need the reigns, but it looked good for the villagers. The fresh bread the last hostess had given him was hard now, but the water was fresh from the spring, and the apple jam helped soften the bread. As Gregory munched the oats in his bag, Jason sat down under a tree to contemplate his next move. Mrs. Brown and her family had been his refuge from the winter storms, but it was spring now, and the mission must be completed. Time was running out. Mrs. Brown was sure that the protectorate by the falls was the last one before the row of artificial jungles. Jason chuckled at the term, thinking how the mind came up with funny ways to call the demise of civilization. He had always called it a jungle out there. She had not heard of a name attached to it, but he hoped it would be the New Hope. If it were not, his journey would continue.

Despite needing a bath and trim, he was striking in appearance and full of vigor. Four and a half years of crossing a continent had toned and tightened his already well-built physic. He had spent the winter keeping in shape, splitting logs for the widow and her neighbors. He had grown to love them, and it had been an emotional goodbye.

"Jason Allen McGregor," she said, standing at the door of her small house, "I don't know what will become of you out there, but you are always welcome back here with or without the twinkle in your eye."

She, of course, did not know it, but she was referring to Jason's best survival trick. One moment you could stare into those dark brown eyes and see his humorous twinkle and read past hurts and wonder who was this fascinating person and the next moment, he was a nondescript face not deserving a second glance. He could blend into the background any time from having been the center of attention, but of course, he had been trained well.

The meager meal completed, he promised Gregory a stall to sleep in tonight and mounted for the last leg of his journey. He hoped privately that they had a good cook Mrs. Brown had not been one. Gregory skillfully found his way down the incline on the fresh spring grass. The early morning fog had lifted, and the air had a fresh mountain smell. Crocuses were blooming wildly at the base of trees, and birds were rapidly building nests. One more time, he hoped in his heart of hearts for success. This was when he thought being a man of prayer would come in handy, but that was not one of his strong points.

Several hours later, he could hear the waterfall plummeting into the crystal-clear lake. The mountain it fell from was the first in a chain traveling south. Jason was grateful he had to go around it, not over it. The castle was in clear view, but the spring breeze was too gentile to raise the banner in the turret. That was too bad; it may have told him something. It was the largest protectorate he had seen, serving the largest group of people living in one area. The potential was rising. The protectorate was a religious Order because he could see the church beyond the castle. As he made his way down the last hill, he headed toward the road that wound through the community and in front of the castle. He passed a field and paused to exchange words with a farmer. He was in his mid-forties and dressed in plain clothing, so he could not tell if he was a villager or a member of the castle community. Gauging his words carefully, he hailed the farmer. "Greetings, sir. How grows the garden on this fine spring day?"

The farmer who had been watching Jason descend into the valley looked up from his hoeing with a look of country indifference mingled with mild curiosity. Leaning on his hoe, he replied. "Well, I won't know till mid-summer and only if it rains enough. You're a stranger to this village, are you not?"

A common enough observation since even this large community could only have three to four hundred people living here at the most. Dismounting so as not to appear superior to this as yet unidentified farmer, Jason extended his hand in greeting. "I am Jason of the western sea, and I have traveled long and through many hardships on my journey. My mount Gregory and I are seeking lodging and refreshment for the night. Does your protectorate take in travelers?"

"Well, met then Jason," the farmer replied, "I am called Jim by the villagers, but my given name is James Farrell." A hearty handshake was exchanged as James continued. "I also am a Brother of the Order and have the authority to welcome you to spend the night or as long as you wish. Walk with me to the barn, and Brother David will see to your mount."

James had slung his hoe over his shoulder and led Jason to the large, well-built barn beyond the field. So far, the greeting was amiable, and Jason started to relax as he led Gregory by the reigns. "So, you say you're from the west," James queried as they walked. "What brings you this far east?"

An understandable question, but Jason did not want to put all his cards on the table yet. "You could call it a pilgrimage, Brother James, and I will know when it's over when I have found what I seek."

"And what would that be? Maybe we could help." was James' sincere reply as a young man, later identified as David, walked out to greet the two approaching the barn.

"I would like to spend some time in your chapel to give thanks for my safe journey thus far" They had reached the barn, and David was taking Gregory's reigns to lead him into the stall. "What is the proper name of your Order so I can give it proper credit in my prayers?"

Jason was not an unbeliever in God in general, but he was not what one would call a believer; the request was a ploy to determine more quickly if he had finished his journey. But unfortunately, he did not realize the emotional and physical drain that had taken its toll or how much he had counted on success this time, so when James responded, "This is the protectorate of the Order of the New Hope," Jason Allen McGregor fainted.

CHAPTER 2

He seemed to be coming out of a deep sleep, but he knew it was not a natural sleep. Voices all around him, too many of them, and Gregory, where was he? Finally, his mental confusion subsided, and logic took over. He feigned continued unconsciousness keeping his breathing under control and controlling facial movements. He could identify James talking.

"I don't know what happened, Richanda. He is a stranger from the west seeking lodging. When I told him the name of our Order, he passed out so fast I could not even break his fall."

A soft feminine voice responded. "His pulse is steady, but I don't have the smelling salts. David, would you run to the dispensary and get my kit? Scott, what do you think?"

The voice that responded was rich and deep, obviously Scott's. "I don't know Richanda, but let's revive him before we try to answer questions. His arrival is curious indeed."

Satisfying himself that no harm was meant to him and not wishing to breathe the smelling salts, Jason fluttered his eyes and visibly woke up.

"Well, well, young Jason, you had me frightened there for a moment. I feared you bought an illness from the west with you." Chimed in, James with a sigh of relief.

Rubbing the back of his neck, hoping to feign a slight concussion later if needed, Jason replied. "It takes more than a little fall to get me down but thank you for your concern. Is Gregory all right?"

The woman laughed softly from behind him, and Jason turned to observe her visually for the first time. He was not disappointed as she was as angelic as her voice. Petite at 5-4 and as trim and in shape as anyone on his old secret service team but with curves in all the right places. Her eyes laughed as well, jumping out of a creamy complexion with soft wavy chestnut hair that fell just below the shoulder. "Your horse is in better shape than you are. But so, like a man, to have his horse as his first concern. Do you think you can stand, or should you sit longer? How hard did you hit your head?" The angelic voice questioned.

Deciding a concussion would be a good idea, he feigned a slight swoon as they tried to get him up. "I am sorry I must have hit my head harder than I thought. Especially because I don't remember your name." And Jason heard that wonderful laugh again.

"I am Richanda Gray Smith, and I oversee the Sisterhood of this community as well as knowledgeable in the healing arts. You have already met James; to your right is Scott Jenkins, head of the Brotherhood. And, of course, you know the man now arriving with my bag David who is caring for your precious horse."

David dropped the bag by her side as if on cue, smiled at Jason tipping an imaginary hat, and retreated into the barn. As Richanda pulled out her blood pressure cuff and stethoscope to take his pressure, Scott took over the conversation. "We do not get many visitors from the west. In fact, we have never had any from beyond the great river. What brings you to us?"

"I would rather speak to your leader concerning that." Jason replied and observed Scott and Richanda exchange glances. She next responded.

"As Scott and I are both second in command and Pastor Carr, the head of our Order, is on the outskirts of the community visiting the sick, you may speak freely with us." Then, with her expressive eyes, she dismissed James, who quietly left to return to his hoeing.

    She had completed a neuro check, and it was time to stand up and finally lay his cards on the table. This time he actually prayed, although he was unsure to who he prayed. Hoping that he had not misjudged the situation or, indeed, his mission would end right here with a grave. "My name is Jason Allen McGregor, and as I said, I come from the west. I represent a small group of people I left behind four and a half years ago in search of a community in the east that was mostly rumor mingled with hope." Both leaders exchanged knowing glances at the last remark. Then, feeling more encouraged, Jason continued. "None of us were television watchers, and after the smashing noticed, we were the only ones to retain both a desire and the ability to remember modern technology. One of the last broadcasts we heard on our short wave, before we lost electricity and all batteries, consisted of an invitation to join a group of "NEW HOPE" in the east. Unfortunately, some of our group died searching too openly, so I was sent. I have had many close encounters with groups I misread. I pray I have not misread you also."

    Richanda smiled quietly, deferring a response to Scott. "Your story Jason is fascinating, and I would like to know more about the west. Also, your natural caution around us is understandable. I have heard of many deaths simply for mentioning the word science. We will talk further about this at dinner. Our noon meal is just past, so Richanda can fix you a bite to eat from the leftovers and give you room to rest and freshen up. Here's David with your saddlebags now. We will supply you with robes of our Order to decrease questions from the villagers. The tower bell will chime five minutes before dinner. I look forward to seeing you then."

Jason stood in disbelief with his mouth partially open as he tried to speak, but Scott was already on his way to the chapel, and Richanda gently guided him to the castle. This was not the response he expected, nor was it the response he feared. Maybe they were also being cautious. He would take his cue from Richanda and wait until dinner. Picking up his saddlebags, he followed her lead, neither speaking as they crossed the field to the castle.

Richanda broke the silence. "The castle was constructed over a three-year span from 1 AT to 4 AT. The chapel, of course, was our original building completed at the time of the smashing with some renovations only just completed."

They had now rounded the first corner, and Jason found himself staring at the shield over the archway with the insignia of the Order. Richanda was watching his response closely. He now knew his journey was over as his heart skipped a beat. The insignia was a perfect square with a pattern inside. Pretty and decorative to a villager but to the discerning eye, a blow-up of a computer microchip. He would allow them to play the game to the fullest as they evaluated his motives, but he now knew the end result.

Passing through the arched portal, he was amazed at the beauty and openness of this castle. This was achieved by the center garden atrium that went up through the structure with no surrounding walls. The columns that supported the structure were gracefully curved hardwoods leading to slightly peaked arches at the top of the ground floor. The foyer area was huge, and the tiles on the floor were well-worn, suggesting frequent use by many people. To his left, the rooms were enclosed so that he could discern nothing. Immediately ahead was the garden. It was lush, green, and well-tended, with crisscrossing pathways leading to all parts of the ground floor. As he looked up to the glass ceiling, he could see balconies on the two middle floors in each room. Beyond the garden was a kitchen to delight any serious cook. However, it still seemed relatively basic and primitive in structure for a group he believed was actually humanity's hope for the future. To his right was a spiral staircase leading to the top three floors. With no dividing walls, the right side consisted of rows of wooden tables and chairs already set for the evening meal. The area in the back, which would have taken up the space of a tower, had small tables for four to six people in clusters.

"Obviously." He stammered, "Your Order is large, or you frequently entertain large numbers of people."

"Actually, neither. We are fairly small, thirty-three adults in number, but we both teach the village children and run a hospital of sorts out of this building. The students who live too far to walk in the winter snows live here also." By this time, the garden had been transversed, and Richanda indicated he should sit down while she sought food. "The cooks will not return for another two hours, so I hope I can find something eatable for you."

Within ten minutes, he was feasting on a meat sandwich made on the freshest bread he had had for a while and drinking actual cold milk. Obviously, there was a refrigeration unit somewhere, but he had not seen it as he watched Richanda prepare his meal.

"This evening, you will eat the meal with Dr. Carr, Scott, and myself at the head table over there." She pointed to a table on a raised platform in the center of the tower room. He nodded understanding as he quickly devoured his lunch. "We do not have private washrooms for guests, but you will be sleeping on the boy's dorm level and can use their facilities. You will, though, have a private room for sleeping. One of the Brothers will lay out fresh clothing for you while you wash. If there is anything else, you need ask anyone, but if anyone asks who you are, you are from the north in our contemplative branch."

Jason nodded his agreement as he finished the cold milk, savoring the sensation. Then, grabbing his saddlebags from him and playing the hostess, Richanda led him up to the middle level and showed him his room. Her closing remark: "Feel free to wander the castle but remember, when you hear the bell, you have five minutes to meet me at the head table."

The shower felt good, proving they had plumbing and a water heater, but the appearance of each convenience had the look of experimental craftsmanship. Maybe the presence of the villagers meant camouflage was needed.

His fresh clothing was comfortable, but instead of exploring as planned, he gave into the call of the bed. He never heard a sound when his clothing was collected for the laundry, nor did he notice his saddlebags missing. The courier headed though not for the laundry but for the chapel. Jason slept soundly.

CHAPTER 3

DR. TIMOTHY BARNES'S fifteen-year-old son Calvin was making his way down the road toward the chapel and the laundry beyond. Of course, the only person who would suspect that he was carrying anything beyond dirty laundry was sound asleep. Although not much stealth had been required, he was glad Richanda gave him the job as it relieved him from English class. Their chapel had been a modest size Methodist church before the smashing, but they had redesigned the inside and enlarged the structure. Inside was a public sanctuary that occupied the bulk of the structure, but a small private chapel was concealed behind the altar. It was to this more secluded area that Calvin headed. He was greeted by the three people he expected Richanda, Dr. Carr, Dr. Scott, and unexpectedly James Farrell.

Richanda saw him first and responded quickly with a smile of approval. "I was beginning to wonder what happened to you. You were not caught, were you?"

"No," The youth replied, "But instead of exploring the castle as you suggested, he took a nap, so I waited to make sure he would not wake."

"Excellent, Calvin, excellent." Responded Dr. Carr. "Take the laundry to the river and bring back any that is dry to hide his bag in when you return."

Calvin quickly exited, knowing he would not be a part of the following discussion, and headed for the end of the lake that formed a stream perfect for washing clothing.

Scott spilled the contents of the saddlebags on the table they were sitting around. His possessions told little, but they suspected as much. A hunting knife, towel, two changes of clothing, soap, carrots for Gregory, two spare horseshoes, nails, hammer, file, compass, notebook with cryptic notes and crude maps, a tinder box, and a ring with a gemstone. His canteen was also just that. They looked over everything in silence, disappointment settling in. Scott broke the mood.

"Nothing here to prove his story beyond what we already know from his name. Sam, are you sure it was listed?"

"Yes, yes, Scott, my eyes are not that old yet. Here you can read the copy for yourself."

Samuel Carr had been a traveling evangelist for the Baptist church at the time of the smashing and, during the formation of their "Order," had been asked to be the figurehead leader of the religious community. Despite his figurehead status, he was still involved in all decisions and discussions, his wise advice gratefully accepted. Deception, however, was not one of his fortes, so he was rarely used for first contact with strangers. Slightly obese with snow-white hair balding at the top, he was the perfect picture of an ancient friar. He enjoyed the freedom of being able to evangelize the community and, at the same time, be involved in saving their mortal minds as well as immortal souls.

The crisp white paper he handed Scott was a list of names produced by a computer, and Sam Carr pointed to the tenth line down, which read:

JASON ALLEN MCGREGOR- OCCUPATION UNKNOWN- RARELY HOME- MARRIED 2 YEARS-WIFE SUICIDE 2 MONTHS AGO- TV COMPLETELY SMASHED- PRESENT WHEREABOUTS UNKNOWN. CONSIDERED DANGEROUS.

The date at the top of the memo listing all area subversives was eighteen months before the smashing.

"Well, James do you have anything to add?" inquired Scott.

"You already know all I observed. However, David did say the horse has traveled far, and his last shoeing was done by an unprofessional, possibly Jason himself."

"Hmmm," Scott replied as he taped his fingers against themselves. "Richanda, how about you?"

"His reaction to the banner was one of recognition, and he loved the cold milk and never questioned the temperature. I feel he is genuine but cautious. It must have been a grueling journey."

"Well then, it's settled. We will confide in him tonight after the children have been dismissed. Those the networks felt to be dangerous and subversive are just the people we are looking for. James, please join Dr. Carr, Richanda, and me at the head table. Invite David and tell him he can bring the lovely Nichole with which he is so enthralled. That is, if we can tear her away from the computer terminal. I want him relaxed during dinner. Ask only normal questions of a villager passing through. Oh, and tell Eric and Ron to disappear for the night. After the meal, everyone resume normal duties, and Richanda will give him a tour, including the library." Her head nodded in agreement. "Sam introduce him to the children with the usual story," the white head bobbed. "James, make sure young Calvin returns the saddlebags as quietly as he stole them. That is all. I will see you at dinner."

There was no further discussion as each went to do their assigned chore. Calvin was disappointed to see James waiting for him on his return journey to pick up the saddlebags he had been hoping for Richanda, as he knew he could get more information from her. But he dutifully slipped the bags in his basket under the clean clothing and made his return trip. He had no problem slipping the bags back in as Jason was sleeping soundly, and Calvin had no wish to wake him yet. Calvin stared at him a moment as he slept and thought to himself that this stranger could be the start of new things at New Hope, and he had better stay close to make sure he was as involved as possible, or he would be stuck in English class forever.

CHAPTER 4

Again, it was hard to wake up, but this time from natural sleep. Someone was rocking his shoulder and calling his name.

"Come on, Mr. McGregor, wake up. It's almost dinner. Richanda sent me up for you."

He rolled over to find a lad he had not yet met grinning down at him. "Who are you?" Asked the groggy Jason.

"I'm Calvin Barnes. My father is the surgeon here, and you are late. Let me help you with your tunic."

"Oh yes, thank you," responded Jason. "Where are my saddle bags? I need something in it before I go down to dinner. And where are my clothes?"

"I stopped in earlier, but you did not wake, so I took your dirty clothing to the laundry (partial truth), and your saddle-bags are here where you left them." (Complete truth- simply omitting the time period they were not there) "Here I'll dump them for you."

Before Jason could intervene, the anxious to please Calvin had dumped the contents on the bed. The ring in question was there, but now he had no way to tell if the bag was searched. He was careless not to have put the ring back on immediately after his shower, and how stupid to fall asleep. What was done was done, and Calvin looked innocent enough with his sandy hair, freckled face, and intense blue eyes.

"Mr. McGregor, they rang the bell a minute ago, and Dr. Carr does not like tardiness. I am to lead you to the head table."

"Very well, Calvin," laughed Jason. "Lead on. Is my tunic on, correctly?"

Calvin nodded in the affirmative as he led Jason to the stairs. If everyone else guarded their conversation around him, Calvin appeared not to. As a result, he was a wealth of information as they descended to the dining area.

"Harvey, one of the farmers and the Dorm Brother, lives in the room across from the one you are using. My Dad lives in the one on the other side of the staircase, and I'm around the corner from you, across from Dad. The men's medical ward is to you're left; that's why Dad and I live here. All the other families with children live in the cottages, but Dad must be nearby in case of a medical emergency."

By now, they had reached the next floor, and Calvin poked his head down the hall, pointing to the room directly under what was Harvey's room.

"That's Sister Cynthia's room. She's the Dorm Sister and secretary. She is also in love with Harvey. The room under Dad's is Dr. Su Lynn's."

They had reached the bottom landing. In the foyer, children were lined up in five rows of ten but not in any apparent age or gender grouping. A Brother or Sister of the Order was in front and back of each line, and the children were singing a hymn before dinner. The woman leading the singing was possibly in her late forties, with dark brown hair with just a touch of gray at the temples. Her eyes reflected wisdom and serenity as her graceful hands led the singing. Although one would not call her a striking beauty, she had an inner beauty that shone out, surpassing physical attributes. Jason's faithful guide continued in a whisper.

"That's Sister Frances, Dr. Scott's wife. She teaches school to the little ones and music. Just don't sing around her, or she will recruit you for the choir." He said with a twinkle in his eye.

Someone who was obviously Dr. Carr walked in from one of the closed rooms and requested God's blessing on the food. Chaos then broke loose as the children scrambled for their chairs. Calvin led him through the throng to a raised table where Richanda and Scott waited. Richanda, with her usual smile of approval, looked at Calvin and said.

"Thank you, Calvin. I hope you and Mr. McGregor are getting along well."

Calvin nodded his agreement and ran off to his seat.

"Come, Mr. McGregor, join our head table." She requested, "You already know Scott, James, and David. The love of David's life right now is beside him, Nichole Peters" Both blushed. "And just arriving is Dr. Carr, our leader."

Both shook hands as they sat down. The conversation around the table was neutral, and they talked of farming and crops and choir rehearsal. Jason talked of traveling and life on the road. The food was sumptuous. A roasted turkey that fell off the bone, fresh vegetables, and tubers of all sorts with fresh bread and rice pudding for dessert. There must be a greenhouse somewhere to get fresh veggies this early in the spring. The wine was excellent and mild, and he noticed even the children drinking the wine. Richanda explained that no safe water purification system was available to the villagers, so wine was the only alternative. Intoxication was rare even in the young. As each finished, they left to go about their own business for the evening, and Jason could not help but notice Nichole and David leaving together until only Jason and Richanda were left.

As they got up from the table so the clean-up crew could take over, she asked. "Would you like a tour?"

"Of course," He answered, and to himself, anything to get some answers.

"Let's start through the kitchen to Dr. Carr's study" They poked their heads in. It was very simply a room lined with bookshelves and a large mahogany desk in the center of the circle formed by the tower. "This is where he prepares sermons and administers church justice and counseling sessions. But, unfortunately, it is also where the children find out what grade they received, so they are terrified of it." The next room heading up the hall to the front was a conference room. They walked in as Richanda explained the various committees that used the room and its use for town meetings as needed. They then proceeded to the library located in the south tower. Again, it was a room filled with bookshelves and a desk, but it also had many comfortable-looking chairs, all unoccupied at present. The desk, however, was occupied, and as they entered, a serious-looking man in his late forties with dark-rimmed glasses rose to greet them. As he stood to his full height of 6-4 and walked to the front of the desk, Jason felt he would not like to meet him in a dark ally until he had brushed up on his marshal arts.

"Hello, Mr. McGregor. I'm Mark Wickersham. I hear you are visiting for a while." They were shaking hands as he heard Richanda lock the door. In an instant, he felt helpless and betrayed as the handshake became a vice grip that he could not break, and even if he yelled, who would hear him? The librarian turned attacker continued. "I forgot to mention that I am the librarian here and in charge of security. We must ensure you are on our side first so co-operate and come with me."

It was not the method he had anticipated. He hoped Richanda had been instructed to seduce him to get information, but that happened only in James Bond movies. This giant bear hug was not what he bargained for.

"Don't worry, Mark," He pleaded. "I have no place to go and no one to call for assistance. I would have hoped you had more faith in your own judgment. I will co-operate fully."

"I'm glad to hear that, Jason, 'cause I like you already," The librarian replied. "But we trusted our judgment once, and

Jessica lost her husband because of it. Richanda, get the door. The others are waiting below."

Jason's back was to the wall that Richanda was heading for, but he clearly heard a swish that could only be caused by electronics, and his heart leaped for joy. Mark loosened his grip, and Jason felt sure he could break out of the hold, but that would accomplish nothing. So instead, Mark gently led him to an elevator. They descended at least three levels, and Mark let him loose in a small empty room save for a chair in the middle. His final words as he headed topside. "Make yourself at home."

As he watched the elevator door close, Jason heard a swishing to the rear. He turned to see the wall disappear, revealing a transparent barrier between himself and some now familiar faces and one unfamiliar. Scott broke the silence.

"Good evening, Jason; please forgive the rough handling, but one can not be too careful these days. So please sit down and do not be concerned for your safety. If we are not satisfied with your answers, we will wipe out your memory for the last 24 hours and place you on your horse heading north tomorrow."

Jason's reply revealed the tension he was feeling. "I appreciate that, Dr. Scott. By the way, what kind of doctor are you?"

Scott smiled briefly, understanding this stranger's frustration. "I am a doctor of psychiatry, and Dr. Carr really is a Doctor of Theology. James was an attorney and political leader, which is why he is usually the one to make first contact with strangers. Richanda, who has just walked in, is a nurse, and Jessica Lane, to my right, is a sociologist. Much of what you say will interest her, which is why she is here. By the way, Mark is a librarian, but his wife Diana was an army sergeant. She taught him everything he knows. Please, Jason, sit down. It may be a long evening."

Jason was still absorbing it all as he sat down. He had not expected such an organized operation or an underground plant. However, these people really did represent hope for the future, and their caution was understood. He had almost lost his life several times at the hands of both villagers and mercenaries. Jessica, a woman in her mid-fifties, was too young to lose a spouse that way. He could feel her sorrow and wondered how long ago it had been. He, too sorrowed each time he, thought of his precious china doll bride. She had been so fragile, and they had crushed her.

After they were all seated on the opposite side of the barrier, Scott continued. "I am the leader of this group, although Dr. Carr's advice is always welcome. He is mainly our representative to the villagers. We are all survivors of the mind-controlling device the networks used and have developed this sanctuary to store human knowledge and dole it out, as the poor, destroyed minds are able to take it in. Despite the apparent peace of our community, we do have our enemies, the survivalist or call them mercenaries, who are scattered in the hills around us. At present, we are at peace with them, but they search daily for evidence that we have technology so they can raise up the villagers against us. We have lost several good people trying to keep our secrets."

Jessica glanced down at the last line, possibly trying to compose herself. Scott continued. "So, Jason, please tell us how you survived the device and how you found us?"

Jason took a deep breath, collected his thoughts, and began his tale covering the last seventeen years. "I will be perfectly open as there is no reason to be otherwise. I am a native of the northeast, but after I graduated from college with a major in criminal law with a side interest in martial arts, I was recruited by the secret service. I was trained in the capital for two years then I received my first foreign assignment to the orient. My cover story was that of a jade dealer as I gathered information to protect our country. My foreign assignment was my salvation as I did not speak the language fluently enough to make television enjoyable, so I sought relaxation elsewhere. I had been there a year when I met my lovely wife, a national named Tee Lee Sung. We courted for the next sixteen months, and she passed the security check. Her love for me kept her from television at the time. The following two years were spent in wedded bliss. The service gives you a year off without spying to establish your cover story with your wife and friends; she never knew I was a spy. We had been married sixteen months, and she was expecting our first child the following spring when I was called to transfer to the west coast office. The general populace may not have been concerned with the death of a few criminals and undesirable, but the service was. My superior felt that my criminology degree would help solve what they called murders.

Despite my fears, my wife adapted well to our society. She was especially enraptured with our TV programming and used it to learn about our culture. I encouraged this past time as I knew I would be out of town frequently. We had just celebrated our second anniversary. The racial migrations were just past their peak, but she felt secure with me. I was then called away to the capital for a high-level meeting. The meeting was important; our organization had discovered that the suicides, although becoming less frequent, were somehow related to the TV. Our best men were working on it, but we were to keep our ears to the ground. I flew straight home to remove our TV set. I never watched it, and I wanted to protect my precious bride. I was too late. I found her in a pool of her own blood. Our child would have been born the next month. It would have been a boy. The coroner called it death at her own hands. I called it murder. In my anger, I smashed the TV set, resigned from the agency, and became a rouge agent with only one goal: find out who murdered my wife and son."

Jason paused then to re-gather his thoughts. His eyes were moist, but he had stopped crying long ago. Jessica was openly crying, and Richanda was on the verge. "I'm sorry, Mrs. Lane. I know my story must cause you grief and open fresh wounds."

She looked up at him with eyes of compassion that needed no verbal response. Feeling comforted, he continued.

"I had enough information to help me track down some leads, but I had not discovered the mastermind behind it all when the war broke out. Because I had not been conditioned, I rejoined the agency and volunteered for troop training. As you know, we never really got into the war full-scale before the truth was known. I led a raid on one of the network's strongholds, and once I was sure they were all in jail and justice would be served, I slipped away and flew home. I moved into a house in the mountains to wallow in my grief as the smashing took place and all technology disappeared around me. I had not grieved my wife and son's loss because I was too busy trying to avenge their deaths, so I sequestered myself away from civilization.

I was living off the land much as the mercenaries do now. In fact, it was mercenaries who found me. Thinking I was one of them, they took me into their confidence. I soon heard the whole sorted history of what had happened over the previous two years. I stayed with them long enough to learn what was happening, but I knew I could not live according to their code of ethics. So I volunteered for a scouting mission from which I never returned, nor did Gregory, the horse I used. I soon found most people to be like the villagers here, and through some difficult lessons learned to be discrete concerning my knowledge of technology. I even had to hide my watch because it had a calculator. Eventually, I headed for the remains of the city. There I found my first high-tech group. Like you, a few had banded together to try to preserve science and knowledge. Our group is not as big, only about fifteen adults and a handful of children, but our purpose is the same. One of our members is a ham radio operator and heard about the "NEW HOPE" but did not know where. So although I was a relatively new member of the group, I was chosen to search for you. I had survival skills, and even being mistaken for a mercenary helped me on my trip. It has taken me four and a half years to find you."

His story complete, Jason sat in silence. Finally, Scott broke the eerie quiet. "That's a fascinating story Jason but what were you supposed to do when you found us?"

"Our group is small and has few resources. We thought if we could find you and join resources, we could benefit each other. Living in the city is dangerous. We were hoping you could take us in." Jason's face reflected the desperateness of his whole group.

Scott thought a moment. "That's all well and good, but how are you to communicate with them and then transport them across the country? One person alone may be able to, but a group with children across that many miles seems impossible to me."

"We have already thought that through. The one valuable resource our group had was a private jet. Mercifully, it escaped the destruction and in our group is a pilot. They will fly to the east coast five years after I left and land at the best airport. Once I found you, I was to construct a communication devise to match the one they have. They are going to land mid-continent to assure communication range. Once contact is made, I will lead them here or some other safe shelter."

It was now Richanda's turn to respond. "Do you have proof of what you say? Why should we trust you?"

Jason quickly responded. "For starters, I know your banner is really a microchip, a fact no villager would readily know, proving I am at least not mind warped. And the gemstone in my ring covers a compartment with several micro dots containing a composite of the information we were able to salvage and plans to build the communicator."

"I'd like to see that microdot, Scott." Responded Richanda, "I think we can trust Jason enough to lift the barrier."

"I agree, Richanda. Jessica, please go and get us some refreshments, and Sam, please go next door to my office and lift the barrier."

Jessica and Dr. Carr got up, nodded toward Scott and Jason, and left the room. Richanda, James, and Scott stood up to welcome Jason as the barrier started to lift. The smiles quickly left their faces as Jason heard the elevator door behind him open. The three were still on the other side of the room, frozen with faces of horror. Jason turned to find not Mark as he expected, but a darkly clad figure looking like a ninja from a B-rated movie with a machine gun poised at the three across the room.

The stranger's left hand rose as demands were made. "I have a grenade armed in this hand, and if anyone moves, I'll blow us all to the devil who spawned you high techs."

Jason's mind worked quickly. The person behind the clothing was average in build, but despite trying to disguise it, the voice was most definitely female. She turned to Jason. "You stranger are obviously a mercenary. I came to rescue you. We have a camp in the mountains and are always ready to welcome one more. I already disposed of the one upstairs, so get in the elevator."

Jason did as instructed, but as his would-be rescuer backed into the elevator, he wrapped his larger hand around the hand holding the grenade and disarmed her with his free hand shouting for help from the three no longer stunned onlookers. Instead, to his surprise, they were laughing and calling to his prisoner.

"Well, Starr, so much for your days of wars and bombings. You don't make a very good terrorist." Richanda laughed.

Scott quickly joined in. "You can put her down now, Jason; she belongs to us. And, don't worry, Mark is all right. Starr is our actress supreme and your final test."

Dr. Carr and Jessica walked in, all smiles carrying the promised refreshments. "I knew you would pass, Jason," Jessica said quietly. "I could tell in your eyes."

Starr was now taking off her outer disguise. She stood about 5-5 in her mid-twenties with short dirty blond hair cut in a wedge shape. Her hazel eyes showed both intensity and mischief at the same time. Jason knew he would enjoy her company.

CHAPTER 5

BELLS WERE RINGING in his head. Why was it always so hard to wake up? Jason could hear the commotion outside as the residents of the castle woke up and prepared for breakfast. Still, in a stupor, he wrapped himself in the blanket and stepped onto the balcony that overlooked the central courtyard. It was still dark, but he could sense the sun trying to come up over the eastern mountain range behind him. The kitchen crew was at work using candles for light. He thought to himself how perfectly they kept up the charade for the benefit of the villagers. He, too, must remember that.

Remember, oh, remember last night. It had been almost morning when they had emerged from the library. Once trust had been established, both sides were greedy for the latest information. Scott and Richanda had poured over the terminal relaying the information on his microdots while Starr, Jessica, James, and Dr. Carr pumped him for information from the west. Jessica was especially interested in the numerous ways each village he encountered had developed, and she took a volume of notes. It was Dr. Carr who finally suggested sleep. The aches and pains in his body told him the little he had was not near enough. Mark was alert and on guard when they emerged from the library. Richanda explained that someone maintained guard in the library as long as someone was below. It would not do, after all, for a villager to see an elevator open up behind a bookshelf.

Jason was bought back to the present by a banging on the door. He opened the door to reveal a tall man with a farmer's tan and physic. Gray was touching the temples of dark curly hair and a short, well-trimmed beard. The smile was quick but genuine as the deep baritone voice greeted him. "Ah, I am glad you are up. I am Harvey, Brother Harvey, the dorm brother" he pointed across the hall to his room as he shook Jason's hand. "Sorry, we did not meet last night. Richanda said if I did not make sure you were up, she would skin me alive."

"I'm pleased to meet you, Harvey, but with all the racket the boys make, I don't know how I could sleep." replied Jason.

"Good, good, glad you're about. Is there anything I can get you?" Jason shook his head in the negative. "Well, I've got to see to the boys then. The next bell is the call to breakfast but watch yourself. The boys stampede the staircase to get in line first." Harvey completed his sentence as he was halfway down the hall, preparing to break up an apparent water fight that was starting.

Jason retreated to his room. A pitcher of water had been placed by the washstand; he would brave the public showers later when he knew the villagers better. It would be wise to take the lead from his new friends as he learned to fit in. The night before, Dr. Carr had announced him as a visiting brother from the north, and no one had had the opportunity to talk with him yet. He was soon refreshed and quickly donned his habit. How clever in its design, the first layer was a comfortable one-piece jumpsuit loose enough for free movement but tailored enough to look uniform. The tunic worn over it was loose, falling just to the knees. The slits on either side allowed free movement, and the belt around the waist was both decorative and practical as various pieces of equipment could be attached to it as needed. The jumpsuits were all gray, but the tunics were various colors. Obviously, there was a system, but he had yet to figure it out.

His tunic was gray, which matched that of the children. He reminded himself to ask Richanda about that.

Again, a bell was bringing him out of his musings as the dorm exploded with the noise of a herd of boys running for the staircase. Harvey had been right. Had he tried to leave then, he surely would have been killed or at least maimed. The other adults on the floor had already gone down, a lesson he would remember, so once again, he emerged from the staircase to observe the morning hymn and prayer. As everyone scattered for their tables, Richanda intercepted him.

"Good morning, Jason. Sleep well?" she said with a cheery smile.

"Well, yes, long enough, no." They both laughed lightly.

"We always rotate who we sit with," she continued, "so please join me as I introduce you to some more members of our community." Richanda led him to the table closest to the kitchen area. All were seated as Richanda took him around to each seat, starting at the head of the rectangular table. "The only person besides Dr. Carr to have a permanent seat is Jenny, our head cook."

A slender woman with long thick hair bound up in a single braid down her back rose and returned his firm handshake. "I'm pleased to meet you, Jason. You met my mother, Jessica Lane, last night. She has yet to go to bed as she woke me this morning to tell me all about you and only stopped because I had to come to cook."

"The pleasure is mine as I've wanted to give my compliments to the cook since last night's scrumptious feast."

"Richanda was right. You are a charmer." Jenny replied with a blush.

"To the left of Jennifer." Richanda continued, "Is Helena Meyers, who assists our librarian."

The handshake was firm but with very delicate fingers, possibly performing precise tasks. She was average in height, but he could not place her age. Her smile was soft and warm and her face youthful, but the salt and pepper hair revealed that she was possibly older than he thought, although she looked his contemporary.

"Good morning Mr. McGregor" She opened.

"Please call me Jason. After all, I became so tightly involved with your boss, Mark, last night. So I think we can drop the formalities."

"I hope you study in the library often, Jason." She countered with a smile.

The man beside her rose to introduce himself with a confident but light handshake. "I'm Benjamin Rose. I'm a concert pianist, so I teach music to the children and work on the farm as long as it does not involve digging with my hands; I need to protect them. Helena is also my sweetheart, so hands off, Jason." Helena blushed, and Ben smiled down on her with undeniable love.

"Don't worry, Ben. I have no intention of seeking romance. Too many ghosts for that."

"Ah, hum," Interrupted Richanda. "Moving away from the two lovebirds and playing host to this table is Paul Welsh, our college professor, and former Olympic equestrian. In other words, he has been taking care of Gregory for you as he oversees the barn."

A hearty handshake was exchanged as the two men sat down to breakfast and ignored the rest seated around the table, talking about horses for a while. It was a hearty breakfast fit for farmers: eggs, bacon, hot cereal, and bread. Jenny certainly was a good cook. As breakfast progressed, he noticed Jenny never got up but from her seat somehow sent signals into the kitchen, and the helpers for the day refilled the platters as they were empty. It was an efficient system, and Jenny certainly was in control.

Richanda finally pulled him away from a favorite topic. "Jason, we sat here for a reason, it is the table furthest away from the children, and Jenny controls when the help passes, some of which are villagers. Here is your cover story." Jason gave her his full and undivided attention. "You are from our only branch in the north. It is four days journey by horse. On the way, you gave away your habit to some poor travelers who had nothing, which is why you are wearing student gray. Your tunic color is tan, and your job up north was animal husbandry. You had three blue stripes in the corner because you were a supervisor. Your new tunic will have two because you are now outwardly assuming Scott's job as head Brother. Scott needed relief to help Dr. Carr. This is why we called you down, but we could not announce it until you accepted late last night. Any questions?"

"Just one." Replied Jason, who had already assimilated the information and was ready to assume his new role. "What does green stand for?"

"Remember Jason. I am a nurse, and it's for the healing arts, yellow is for education, lavender is for the arts, and tan is for agriculture and animals. The two jobs are combined when there is a second color as a border on the hem. For example, Ben being a concert pianist is lavender, but he teaches, so there is a yellow band at the hem. Not everyone is really what their color suggests, but it works for the villagers."

"Quite a nice system. Do I assume white is for the clergy?" Jason queried, inclining his head toward Dr. Carr.

"Of course, he wouldn't have it any other way." Answered Helena with a grin.

The meal was over, and Dr. Carr rose for the morning announcements. Jason was amazed at how quiet the students became as soon as he stood up. This was a well-disciplined school. Dr. Carr must have been a good evangelist in his day as his voice carried well to every corner of the sizeable semi-opened area.

"I would like your attention, please. Last night I told you that Brother Jason had arrived from the north. This morning I am pleased to inform you that he has agreed to change his assignment from supervisor of animals up there to head Brother here at the main branch of our Order." On signal from Richanda, Jason stood up, and the room exploded in applause. Dr. Carr continued as Jason sat down. "We called him down to consider this post as Brother Scott will be assisting me and will not have time to oversee the Brotherhood properly. We will renovate Brother Scott's office, and Jason will move there. For curious eyes, Jason is not a novice or a student but, in the tradition of our Order, gave all his clothing to the poor as he traveled down, keeping only travel clothing. His new habit denoting his new responsibilities will be ready soon. If you see him during the day, introduce yourself and welcome him. Thank you. Students and staff, you may be dismissed for morning chores."

With amusement, Jason noted they were not as quick to run to their chores. Some of the older children stopped by his table for a quick greeting and then rushed off. Some headed for the kitchen as part of the clean-up crew, some to the garden and started weeding. A few went to the library under the supervision of Helena and two groups up the stairs under the watchful eyes of Harvey and someone who must be Sister Cynthia as she had her arm tightly wrapped around Harvey.

Richanda followed his gaze and smiled. "We don't know what to do when the two of them decide to marry. They are excellent dorm parents."

"It looks like they better make it legal soon, or your religious Order may soon have a bad reputation."

"Don't worry, Dr. Carr is counseling them, and this religious Order is as much for our protection as anything. They won't endanger everyone unnecessarily. But come, Jason, it's time you learned the ropes. While the children are cleaning, there are no restrictions on the floor."

"In other words, I should not try to shower during clean-up, or a ten-year-old may pop her head in on me," Jason replied with a twinkle in his eye.

"Very correct," laughed Richanda as she led him up to the first level. She turned to the right at the top of the stairs and started down the hall. "To the right is Cynthia Black's room. Recognize the name?"

"Olympic archer, wasn't she? Won the gold in the last Olympics before the smashing, if my memory serves me correctly." Jason responded.

"Correct." Richanda smiled. "Your memory is good. She was also a secretary, so she looks after the girls and the books. Underground she does data input and defense training. We are all good with a bow and arrow." Her voice lowered to almost a whisper on the last line. She continued. "We always try to keep the three rooms across from the dorm parents empty for visitors or new students we want to keep an eye on." A knowing glance was cast at Jason; he thought that he had been well supervised during his stay.

"Continuing down to the right is the women's medical ward. Dr. Yamoto will give you a tour later." Rounding the corner, he could hear the children cleaning the privy and complaining as only children can. "The two rooms on the right are private medical rooms. The walls on the ward and rooms are soundproof, so the children do not bother the sick. Jenny is in the last room on the right, and her room has a spiral staircase in the corner leading to the kitchen. It only leads to the kitchen and is not hidden, so the children know about it." She smiled at that statement, and Jason felt there must be other staircases the children did not know about.

"The corner room is our classroom. For first through sixth grade, classes are non-formal and held all over the castle or on the grounds. We stress skills vs. bookwork. Only the children who show self-motivation goes on in book studies beyond a sixth-grade level."

"Are you not going against your goal then?" Queried Jason.

"Not really. Until recently, all our students except protectorate children were mind-warped. They had no desire for knowledge or technology, and we did not want to arouse the villagers' suspicion. However, some of last year's students are eating up the books as they seek the knowledge we will direct them. Some day a child from here will re-discover electricity." All the rooms that face the balconies are for dorm rooms to give the students more room. They are small, with two to three students per room.

"Your ambitions are high. I can see why you choose the name New Hope but what is this room now?"

"That is the sewing room where your new tunic is being made, and the next is a study room. Since the dorm rooms are small, they come here to study. The corner room is mine. At the doorway is my office where I administer dorm and Sisterhood business."

They had walked in the door, and Richanda made a hand sweep to include the whole room as she spoke. "In the back right-hand corner is the door to my bed chamber. The layout is identical to what your room will be." They again stepped out into the hall. "Nichole, Starr, and Su Lynn occupy these last three rooms. Shall we head to your floor?"

"But of course," Jason replied with a bow and a flourish, pointing to the staircase.

"The basic layout is identical, and I'm sure you know your hallway." Jason nodded. "We will head to your new room. To our left is Dr. Barnes's room; of course, you know where Calvin sleeps. David's is next, and Ronald Schmidt, our engineer and choir director, is in the room before yours. But you will learn more about him later. Ben Rose has the room next to the classroom, and the sewing room is a wood shop up here. Now to your new office."

The rooms were almost identical, but Richanda's had a more lived-in appearance. Scott was very precise and methodical as everything had a place and was resting in its place. Richanda pulled a key out and headed for the corner door.

"We keep these doors locked at all times. Remember that Jason never leave it unlocked." Richanda glared at him with a stern look to emphasize her point.

"Yes, Ma'am." He replied with a mock salute.

"It's no laughing matter, Jason. I'll show you."

Once inside the room, Richanda locked the door. There was a bed and a chest of drawers but nothing else.

"Scott lives in a cottage with his wife and two youngest children. We are glad you are here to help occupy this important room." Richanda walked to the closet, explaining as she played with some decorative woodcarving. "This room and mine are also completely soundproof. I'll teach you the sequence of movements needed to activate the computer later." A small panel suddenly moved to one side, and Richanda placed her palm against it. "Computer confirm identification."

A voice defiantly female but also impersonal computer came from the wall.

"RICHANDA GRAY SMITH VOICE AND PALM PRINT CONFIRMED"

"New identification to be processed signal when ready." Richanda replied.

"READY TO ACCEPT IDENTIFICATION"

Richanda took Jason's hand and placed it against the panel, which shone red momentarily, then green.

"READY TO ACCEPT VOICE PRINT STATE FULL NAME"

"Jason Allen McGregor." Said Jason boldly.

"VOICEPRINT ACCEPTED AND LOGGED TO MATCH PALM PRINT. RICHANDA GRAY SMITH STATE SECURITY CLEARANCE TO BE ASSIGNED JASON ALLEN MCGREGOR."

"Full clearance unlimited access," responded Richanda. "Open the elevator, please."

Richanda looked at Jason and smiled. I know it is just an AI, but I like to say please and thank you for keeping up the formalities.

A panel beside the closet opened to the side, revealing a metal door, and Jason could hear the motor as the elevator came up. He then realized this was in the same position as the elevator in the library. When finally, the door opened, they stepped in.

"This is the top floor as the elevator mechanism corresponds to the next floor. The only way to get to the elevator from these top floors is voice and palm print. The computer will also tell you who is below and will give you simple information and data retrieval. Also, if you forget to lock your door, opening the elevator door automatically locks it."

Richanda closed the door, and Jason got his first real look at the control panel being too tired last night. His room was level two; Richanda's level one and the library ground. Then followed negative numbers indicating underground levels going down to negative six. Quite a complex, he thought.

"The children are all in a class by now, so they will not notice that we do not return from your room. We will go underground where Scott will meet us." Richanda pushed negative four, and they descended quietly.

CHAPTER 6

SCOTT, NICHOLE, AND Helena were on level negative three. Nichole was sitting in the middle, hands poised over the computer keyboard. All three had their eyes riveted to the screen.

"Do you want a printout on this, Scott?" questioned Nichole.

"That would be nice." He glanced at Helena with a questioning look in his eyes. "One for you too?" Helena nodded and turned her attention back to the screen. No one spoke as the computer and printer did their job. When completed, Helena grabbed for her copy like a greedy child who had found the perfect play toy.

"I still can't believe this design." she exclaimed, "An electronics expert must have designed it. The plan is simple and basic anyone could put it together, but the functions are complex. A long-range beacon, short-range verbal communicator on a frequency no radio could pick up."

"Are you saying," Scott broke in, "that it will work as Jason said?"

"Oh yes." Beamed Helena. "And even better for our use. Julie can take it with her on her ocean treks, and the groups that go foraging in the city can use it. And you really can start a northern branch and stay connected with them. Mercenaries will never discern this frequency with the antiquated equipment they use. So think of the potential."

"I am Helena. I am." Replied Scott as he pondered momentarily. "Well, off you go to your little shop. I know you can't wait to start on a prototype." Helena was halfway down the hall as he spoke, still speaking to herself. "Nichole, I want you to input everything from those microdots to the puter. Only come up for air and eat a meal or two with us."

"Yes, Brother Scott," she said, emphasizing the Brother. "I'll try not to be too cloistered. Send Cynthia down. She can speed up the work."

"As soon as classes begin, and she can leave the office." He glanced at the digital readout on the wall. "Oh, my goodness, classes have started, and I'm to meet Jason and Richanda. Signal Cindy yourself. She's in Dr. Carr's office. I must be off."

As he rushed out the door, Nichole laughed softly to herself. It was not like Scott to be forgetful, but then they had not had this much excitement in a long time. Yes, she was grateful to this stranger from the west. The group was getting stagnant, starting to behave like a religious Order forgetting their goals and purpose. Maybe he could stir things up a bit. She loved everyone dearly, but a cloistered nun, she was not. Well back to work.

CHAPTER 7

JASON WAS BOTH amazed and pleased with the underground plant. It was basic and utilitarian with no wasted space, and yet it seemed each area had a touch of personality from the person who worked there. Some rooms were like an immense museum housing such things as blenders, curling irons, washers, and dryers, all being preserved as models for a future technological society. Richanda had given him a tour of only one floor before going to Scott's office one floor up for more orientation. His office was the control center for the community, with a large, illuminated map showing the castle and all surrounding buildings on one wall. Certain areas seemed to be rigged to an alarm system, which produced a visual display on the map. The next wall contained a detailed map of the entire underground facility. Green dots were illuminated at each spot a warm body was, and Richanda laughed as she watched one spot move quickly down the hall.

"That must be Scott realizing he's late."

At that moment, Scott burst into the room, slightly out of breath but all smiles. "Jason, your here. I knew Richanda would never be late. She has an uncanny inner clock."

There was an informal grouping of comfortable but functional chairs near the only wall without a map, and Scott indicated the group should sit there. Scott produced a packet of papers on a small central table, looked at Jason, and smiled. "Well, Jason, we have a long morning ahead of us. To adequately deceive the villagers, we need to know exactly what route you took to arrive here, and you need to know how to act like a Brother. First of all, look at these two pictures. You have not met either one yet as they were purposely kept away."

Jason found himself looking at blow-ups of two men both in their early to mid-forties. The first had dark curly hair, blue eyes, a cleft in his chin, and a very intense expression.

"This is Eric Richter. He is a farmer above ground and is divorced with three children. They all came here to live four and a half years ago. His oldest lives in the village and is married to a villager. His mind is intact, but he is unaware of the underground as he is married to a mind warped. Fritz and Hans, however, are high-tech and live in a cottage with their father just on the edge of our property closest to the village. Eric is a nuclear physicist, but he doesn't do much of that. He is our demolition expert, though.

The second man is Ronald Schmidt he is single and a general handyman up top. He's an engineer and made many of our recent additions. He has been with us for two years. Study these pictures well as both men have the cover story of coming from the northern community." Jason now studied the pictures with more interest. Ronald was blond, blue-eyed, and kept his hair closely cropped. He had a neatly trimmed beard, which made him look like a member of a religious community, but he had a look of mischief in his eyes.

"When you meet these two at lunch, the villagers expect you to know one another," Scott continued. "Eric and Ron are well loved by the villagers, so by being friends of yours, you should have no problem fitting in. Also, our "branch" up north is reported to be small, so you should know each other well. So I will expect an exuberant reunion. Oh, and by the way, Eric was just up north visiting two months ago." With a twinkle in his eye,

Jason shook his head in the affirmative. "Good, that part out of the way. Let's get down to the day-to-day routine."

The rest of the morning dragged by with Scott droning on about the routines of community life, Brotherhood responsibilities, which of the children could be trusted, and which of the children had access to the lower level. Jason was amused to see Calvin Barnes on the list. Three hours later, he was relieved to see Richanda enter with iced drinks and something for his headache, although he did not remember her leaving.

"Either you read minds or operate on a very empathic level. This is just what I needed." Jason said as he accepted the drink and pill.

"Scott swears it's my nursey compassion, but I've always picked up strongly on emotions." Richanda then raised her glass in a salute to Scott and then Jason. "Cheers and enjoy. Iced drinks are only enjoyed below." Jason smiled and gave her a wink as he drank the cool lemon-flavored drink.

"Thank you, Richanda, for reminding me of how I drone on." laughed Scott. "Why don't you raise the wall and let Jason relax with my one luxury down here."

As he spoke, Richanda rose and pushed a button on the empty wall near the corner. The entire wall rose, revealing an aquarium large enough to please any marine biologist and filled with a breathtaking variety of fish. Jason lost himself in the tranquility of the swimming fish until Scott interrupted his peaceful respite.

"Quite impressive, is it not." Jason shook his head in the affirmative. "Julie, our marine biologist, spends most of her time there when not making treks to the shore. They represent the best we could rescue from all the major aquariums in the area. We had to work fast after the smashing, as no one was willing to enter a city even to save fish. We released all the fish and mammals that could survive in the local ocean and fresh water, but these beauties needed more special conditions, so we pilfered the largest tank and prepared them a home. Before the tank was completed, everyone had fish tanks in their rooms and homes. I just sit here and stare and hope to forget the pressures of the day. Be careful, though. It can be as hypnotic as the device only, not as destructive."

A loud but obnoxious ringing broke the peaceful repose throughout the entire complex. "That." Explained Richanda. "Is our warning that we have forty-five minutes to make our way upstairs for lunch. Always go up the same way you came down. The villagers are mind warped regarding technology but are not stupid, and if you enter the chapel and suddenly appear from the castle, they will become curious."

As they arose to leave, Richanda continued her orientation. "There are five elevators. One, of course, leads to the library and our rooms, also, as you may have guessed, to the chapel." Jason nodded his head. "A third one comes up in a cavern behind the falls, and the other two lead to Scott's home and the Wickersham's."

At this point, they had reached an intersection, and Scott waved as he headed south to his home exit. Jason and Richanda continued until they met up with Nichole and Helena at the main elevator. Nichole was already interrogating the computer.

"Computer, is the library clear of nonessential personal?"

"YES"

Richanda next asked. "Has anyone knocked on Richanda's or Scott's door since 0700?"

"NO"

She continued, "Is anyone in the hallway outside of those rooms?"

"NO"

She turned to Jason. "Good, we can leave as we came."

As the elevator door opened, Jason bowed with a flourish. "Ladies, after you, please."

All burst into laughter as the elevator took them to their respective floors. Jason bobbed into his guest room to freshen up and, for once, was in the main foyer before the singing started.

CHAPTER 8

As Jason made his way to the table, he heard his name proclaimed loudly. "Jason, when did you arrive?"

He turned to see Ronald and went into his award-winning act putting on a big smile and much back thumping. "Ron, is that really you? Still fixing everything that breaks?"

Ron nodded his head and started guiding Jason to a side table. As they approached, Eric stood and turned towards them. The same scene was repeated as everyone sat down for lunch. They had been just as well briefed as he had been, and when the village server bought over the soup, tureen Eric clearly but not awkwardly said. "I understand you took the scenic route down, as I suggested. Any problems?"

Jason replied. "No, it was wonderfully refreshing, as you said on your last visit. But did you ever think I would move down here too?" Both shook their heads.

It was a simple statement, but when Elise heard her husband grumbling about the stranger that night in the village pub, she reported, feeling very good about her detective skills, that the other two northerners knew him. She further stated that he had even followed their instructions on how to get here. Her honesty and integrity convinced the others, and word soon spread that Brother Jason had been with the Order from the beginning. Some even swore they had heard about him before his arrival. The villagers at least accepted his story and questioned no further. Charles McAllister, who lived on the outskirts of the village, was not as easily convinced. He kept his concerns to himself as he unobtrusively sipped his brew each night at the pub.

BOOK II

CHAPTER 9

SUMMER WAS NOW upon the village. It was still cool at night in this higher altitude, but the days were warm, if not too warm. James' garden flourished, and he had an excellent tomato crop. Although they were still on the green side, Jenny was already contemplating a day of canning to preserve them for the long winter as she walked by the garden. She was followed in single file as if she led a parade by the women of the Order and several children laden down with empty baskets, blankets, and buckets. The sun was barely up, and they were headed to the foothills to berry pick. Although an essential task to provide fresh fruit, jams, and preserves for the group, Jenny always made it a fun task and bought her organizational skills from the kitchen to the fields.

The berries were wild but always bought a good harvest, and Jenny's jams were highly praised among the villagers. This was the first time the Wells twins had come on a berry pick, but Alex had insisted they had a lot of stamina for five years old and would do well. Jenny had Aleshia by the hand so Alex could keep track of Gillian and her son Christopher. At least she thought she had Aleshia's hand. They were so identical only Alex and John could tell them apart.

They arrived at the picnic spot, and Jenny divided the group into an efficient workforce. Christine Jenkins, a younger version of her mother, paired off with her best friend Sharon Farrell and agreed to oversee the two older Fitzgerald children. Although

Jenny suspected that they would go to a secluded spot and talk boys, she hoped that having Frank Jr. along would keep them productive if just to show off. Cynthia joined Alex to help with the twins and Christopher. Sandra-Jean took her two youngest and joined Starr in a nearby area. Frances waved goodbye to her daughter and went with Diana to help keep her three children picking instead of fighting. Finally, Nichole and Jenny were left in the clearing to prepare for the first batch to return.

They spread blankets near the stream, and buckets were filled with water so that when twelve-year-old Dan Fitzgerald came running down the hill with two full baskets of blueberries and a blue ring around his mouth, they could start the process of washing and sorting. Naturally, only the good berries went home, and some good berries never made it to the final basket. As they sat under a large shade tree by the stream side, the two lapsed into comfortable conversation. They were close friends being close in age but rarely saw one another. Cooking responsibilities prevented Jenny from going below often. Of late, Nichole rarely came up for air, which undoubtedly reinforced to the villagers that she was the devout semi-cloistered Sister who prayed for the souls of men in the chapel.

"So, Jen, what do you think of Jason?" Queried Nichole with a smile of conspiracy.

"Nichole, you are as bad as Sharon and Christine talking boys already." The two laughed as Jenny continued with a sigh. "Oh, I don't know, but I think Richanda has her sights on him. Although I wouldn't mind taking a moonlit walk around the lake with him." Jenny's face took on a dream-like appearance with a slight smile of pleasure at the thought. "But enough of my dreams. When are you and David announcing your wedding?"

"David is ready, and so am I, but Pastor Carr wants to wait until after the harvest is in to announce it. Seems Scott wants a pre-winter wedding to provide a cover story for the group from the west to come down and get to know us. There is also a problem with where we will live. Apparently, David will not be around to build our cottage. I don't know where he will be, but Scott said he would be gone till harvest."

Jenny responded sympathetically. "That is a tough problem. What will you do if David can't build you a house?"

"Oh, don't worry, I have something up my sleeve if all else fails. I don't want to wait any longer than I must, but I have no choice at this point. Sometimes when David gets too passionate, it's hard to wait, but a pregnancy is too hard to hide even for a cloistered sister and protection too unreliable."

"Why, Sister Nichole, you sound absolutely scandalous." Laughed Jenny.

"Don't I just." And the two continued laughing and sorting berries.

They had not noticed the well-camouflaged Charles McAllister, who was in a blind by the stream fishing. He had constructed the blind, not that the fish needed it, but to keep Casey's gang from harassing him and making his catch their own. He had not expected the revelations in this conversation, but it certainly put some more pieces into the puzzle he was making in his mind. It was still too early to tell Casey, the self-appointed leader of his group. He would bide his time; they all thought him weak because he lived so close to the village, but he knew it would pay off. He just had to make sure his timing was right. The girls said nothing else of interest, and he was glad of the arrival of the team with the carts and more baskets and the long-awaited and well-deserved picnic lunch. Charles used the confusion to slip away. He was observed as he left, but Calvin Barnes did not think much of it but remembered it.

CHAPTER 10

THE SUN WAS setting behind the mountains as the berry pickers loaded onto the carts for the return ride. It took two large carts drawn by the Clydesdale horses from the barn to lug the team and their berries. The reward for a full day's work was a leisurely ride back and a bonfire cookout waiting for them. Calvin and Jason led the teams really slow. The twins were fast asleep, and as the adults reflected on a beautiful summer day, the children sang choruses they had learned in Bible class. The castle staff had prepared the buffet, spread out on planks in front of the castle. As guests of honor, the berry pickers were the first in line for the feast. Alex and John went to put the twins to bed, and by the time they returned, Christopher was already on his second course. Jenny had left a competent crew to cook, and everyone was in a festive mood.

After everyone was stuffed full of tender meats, fresh fruits, vegetables, and fresh from the oven bread, the children went down to the lake to watch the floating fire David and Paul had constructed. It had been a private dinner party, but the evening of dancing was open to all, and as the bonfire was lit, the villagers gathered for an evening of dancing, music, and storytelling.

A band formed between the castle musicians and the villagers, and the dancing started. Jason was his usual charming self and danced with everyone, including the village grandmother

Mrs. Cowman. It was some time before Richanda was able to have him to herself.

"Jason, where have you been lately?" She gasped as he twirled her around.

"Busy, my dear Richanda. I have been busy doing the business of the Order." Jason laughed in return.

They had finished the swift-moving dance, and both walked off hand in hand toward the far side of the lake for some quiet conversation. Jenny was being swept off her feet by Ron and never noticed that Richanda was getting her moonlit walk. Richanda broke the silence.

"Well, Jason, you still have not answered my question. Where have you been? I've been busy in the hospital wing, but I still make it for meals, which you rarely do lately."

"Ah, I see Scott does not tell all his plans even to you," Jason replied as he looked into her eyes with affection and mischief at the same time. "Calvin and I have been out on hunting expeditions purportedly to bring in meat for the winter, but in reality, we have been seeking a suitable place for the northern community."

"Have you been successful in your hunting?"

"Not much meat but a beautiful spot for a new community. And don't feel so put out you would have found out at tomorrow's staff meeting." He gave her a friendly shoulder hug, quickly becoming the full passionate hug Richanda had hoped for. "My my Sister Richanda, I have been spending too much time with Calvin."

They laughed softly as they continued their journey, walking closer together than before.

CHAPTER 11

It was not a usual staff meeting, and the conference room was completely filled. Scott and Jason sat at the head of the table with a large map on the wall. Richanda was beside Scott, feeling slightly miffed that she did not know all those two had been up to. The only other person who knew the reason for the meeting was Calvin, who felt very proud of himself. Also present were Nichole Peters, David Douglas, Alexandria and Jonathan Wells, Helena Meyers, Frank Fitzgerald, Michael Alden, Ron Schmidt, Diana Wickersham, and Harvey Stots. When Scott stood, the room became silent.

"I have exciting news for you all. You may have wondered why Jason and Calvin have been missing lately. They have been combing the general northern region looking for a place to settle our future western visitors, and they have had success."

Everyone clapped, and those sitting near Jason and Calvin expressed warm congratulations. Scott continued.

"The spot is less than four days journey and by all evidence has been vacant since the smashing. There is evidence of villages encroaching on the area, but the nearest is at least a day and a half journey away, and the people don't appear to travel beyond their village. Some rocky mountains surround it, so it is not a convenient route for travelers, traders, or even mercenaries. I am proposing we build a smaller version of ourselves up there for them. Frank, Jason was able to get some good photos, which he handed out, and Nichole should be able to come up with some good computer graphics on the topography. Can you draw up some working plans?" Frank nodded and started sketching on a pad. "Helena, there is a waterfall nearby and plenty of sun to set up some solar panels. I don't want you to travel up there, so construct all they will need and teach Ron how to set it up."

"Still protecting me, Scott?" Helena said with a smile.

"Yes, of course I am. You are too special a person to risk."

"Don't worry, Scott, I'll fill the bill, and if their electronics wizard is as good as his designs indicate, they will have no trouble improving and expanding."

"Ron, I want you and David to go out tomorrow and start excavating the underground plant. Take my son Steve and Fritz Richter as workhorses. I think three levels underground should be sufficient for the size of their group, and we have all the important prototypes stored here anyway."

"One question." Ron interrupted Scott's monologue. "How do we find this place if we don't take Jason or Calvin? I flunked pathfinder 101 in boy scouts."

"Forgive me for rambling on." Intoned Scott. "Jason left one of the homing beacons under a tree. You can follow it up to test how the beacon will work when our friends arrive. Jason will also draw you a general map." Ron nodded, apparently satisfied. "There are some pre-existing buildings that have survived the seasons. Try to use them. Michael, we can't let everyone go north. Our villagers would get suspicious, so make your plans now, and we will send you up later to camouflage the electronics. Harvey, we will send you with Michael to do some of the finish work. Alex, you will oversee the medical wing as Richanda will care for any accidents." Alex and Richanda exchanged knowing glances as Scott continued.

"The cover story for your mass exodus will be an evangelical crusade. As an experienced teacher, Jonathan will go with Dr.

Carr to help lead the meetings. We will hold legitimate meetings in all the villages surrounding the area to help establish our Order's presence as the villagers encroach the area. Diana, you will stay with Sam and Jonathan as extra security as they travel. Jason and Richanda will lead the work crews. Ron and Dave will leave tomorrow for a hunting trip. The rest will leave in four days, giving you enough time to prepare. I want the whole group to stay together until you are well beyond the local area."

"Jonathan, Diana, when you interact with the locals, let them know the general area of the Order but do not give specifics. I want the northern community to be well established by the time they are discovered. And remember, whatever you construct should look at least five years old. Any questions?"

"Just one." Piped in David, "When do you want this little miracle done?"

"We start looking for Jason's friends in mid-September and hope to bring them there by the end of October, depending on how far away they land. I only need a shell for the underground plant and a castle above. They can survive the winter with the basics and improve on them next spring. Jason reports a fair size city five miles north of the spot, which explains why the area is deserted and avoided, but you may find some motorized help there. What say we plan an engagement party for when you return with the job done?"

"I say that's a pretty good incentive to work fast, Scott." As David grinned from ear to ear, Nichole blushed and held his hand tightly.

As Scott paused for further questions, Frank looked up from his sketch pad, already filled with preliminary plans, and spoke as if no other conversation had occurred since Scott gave him his marching orders, so engrossed was he in his plans. "Scott, do you want a fish tank in the main office for when you visit?"

The whole room laughed, and Scott actually looked momentarily embarrassed, realizing how well-known his passion for his fish was. "No, Frank, I can be away from them from time to time. We will let them install their own vises. Any other questions?" Scott queried as he looked over the group and could see other minds beyond Franks working on plans for the future.

"Only one problem Dr. Scott." The question came from a slightly timid yet slightly overconfident Calvin. "What is my job to be in all this? Surely you're not leaving me behind just when it gets fun?"

Scott thought a moment. "To be truthful, Calvin, I had not thought of how to use you. But, Jason, it was your idea to take Calvin hunting. Where do you feel he can best be used now?"

Calvin turned to Jason and pleaded with eyes more expressive than words. Although Calvin loved his father, he rarely saw him, and Jason had become a role model hero to an impressionable boy maturing into a man.

"Well, now, Scott." Jason began, "We could use him as a workhorse with Steve and Fritz, but I think he would be dead in a week." The whole table laughed as Calvin's aversion to manual labor was well known. Although he was not lazy, just not muscular and preferred to use his head in most situations. "I think." Jason continued. "That we could best use Calvin as a messenger between the two teams. We have a communicator to keep in touch with you, but Dr. Carr doesn't dare carry one. Calvin knows the area well, and as I learned on my first day here, he is good at half-truths and deceptions." Again, good-natured laughter filled the room. "He is also good at discerning character and will be valuable in discovering the attitudes of the villagers Dr. Carr speaks to."

"Excellent idea Jason." Scott said with a special grin for a now embarrassed Calvin. "If there are no further questions, we should dismiss there are already too many of us below at one time. Make sure you go up in small groups. We don't need suspicion now."

As the group rose to leave, Scott motioned for Jason, Richanda, and Calvin to stay behind. When the room had cleared, Scott put his arm around Calvin and looked down on him. Not that Calvin was short, but Scott's six-foot-eight frame made everyone short. "Calvin, I'm pleased with Jason's suggestion of how to use your special abilities, and I'm pleased with your willingness to help, but what has been suggested can be dangerous, and I want you to understand that before you agree."

Calvin tactfully broke from Scott's fatherly grasp and stood as tall and proud as he could. Then, looking Scott straight in the eye, he responded. "Sir, I saw what happened to Mr. Lane and Mr. Myers, and I also saw what happened to the stranger three years ago who tried to use a calculator in the market. I know the dangers out there, but if I'm to become an adult, my dad can be proud of it's time I started facing the realities of life and not just hiding in the walls of the protectorate."

"Well said, Calvin," Scott replied. "Had your father heard you, he would be proud. But, you are still his son and not yet in a position to determine your complete destiny, so I will ask your father if you can go. Now off with you and help David in the stables. I want you to be able to shoe your horse if you must."

"Yes, sir," Calvin replied with a grin as he ran off suddenly back to the young boy with no cares in the world.

Scott sighed. "Youth, what I wouldn't give to be young again, and yet I wouldn't want to go through it again. Now then, Jason and Richanda, we have some plans to make. Richanda, Jason tells me you felt left out. Forgive me, but with all the babies being born, I felt you had your hands tied up too much to worry about preliminary plans."

"I'll let you go this time, Scott." Richanda laughed. "I just don't want this upstart from the west taking over my position." They all laughed as Richanda poked Jason in the ribs. Their meeting lasted straight to dinner, but with few villagers around, no one noticed their absence.

CHAPTER 12

Tim Barnes had his reservations over Calvin's involvement in the construction crew, but he also recognized that Calvin needed to sprout his wings. It had been hard raising Calvin alone. His mother had died giving birth to his stillborn sister when he was not quite six. The last seven years at the protectorate had been good as all the women took it upon themselves to look after Calvin, but even Tim had to admit he was on the verge of adulthood, so he gave his blessing.

Sam Carr was in his glory. He hadn't had an actual successful evangelical meeting since before the device was used and was anxious to dust off some of his favorite bring them down the aisle weeping sermons. Although he was only the cover story, he planned to attack his job with righteous fervor. He felt sorry for Scott, although a believer was not a preacher and would have to deliver the sermons in his absence. Oh, how he wished he could be a church mouse to see his first one.

Richanda had more than likely been the busiest of them all. Alexandria Wells was an excellent nurse who took her duties seriously, but she had three children and did not live in the castle. Su Lynn was a tremendous help and agreed to take over Richanda's night call, but Richanda still had a lot to do to leave things running smoothly. Starr and Cynthia took crash courses in medical emergencies and home delivery and were then available to assist in the medical wing. The men's ward was essentially empty, but the women were still having babies, and Richanda felt guilty leaving. Still, she couldn't pass up the excitement or the opportunity of possible time alone with Jason. He was an enigma she needed to figure out, and she planned to have fun doing it. What she wouldn't give for a young girl who was not mind warped to train in the medical arts.

David and Ron had successfully left for their hunting trip heading west to throw off suspicion. Steve and Fritz were seeking sympathy from everyone who would listen to all the demanding work they would be subjected to. Frank and Nichole were excited about the new challenges and worked night and day to complete the architectural plans. Helena did not have time to complete the generator but sent two solar panels and promised the rest in one month. Jason and Calvin took long rides each day to improve Calvin's horsemanship and his ability to travel unnoticed. Jason spent time telling Calvin stories of his secret service days and some of the close calls he had had, and how he got out of them. Calvin was unaware of it, but Jason was training and hopefully preparing him for his job. Calvin thought it was great spending time with Jason and getting to know Ginger, the speckled mare he had been given.

And so, the day came to leave. Dr. Carr gave his congregation a sermon of encouragement, and they all stayed after to help pack. The vital equipment had been packed the night before, but the villagers loaded up the food, teaching materials, and canopy Dr. Carr would use for the meetings. They took two covered wagons that looked more like houses on wheels and made the group look like gypsies of old. It was a festive occasion dampened only slightly by the soft summer rain, which started falling during church.

Charles McAllister was highly interested in the events of the day. He had planned on following the hunting expedition, but they headed west, and he knew Dr. Carr's group was heading north, so he changed his plans. It was then he regretted that he didn't have a co-conspirator to help, but that would mean he would have to share the glory of his knowledge with someone, and he did not want to do that. After all, if he could cause the downfall of this protectorate, maybe he could take away the leadership from Casey and move into the castle.

He pondered these glories and the thought of Casey serving him dinner on a silver platter as he stood by the road watching the wagons go by. He was a nondescript person and was rarely noticed, so he thought nothing of his observation post, seeing himself as just another villager. On the other hand, Calvin was practicing his observation skills. He focused on Charles because he was not a member of the congregation and because he had seen him recently fishing near the berry pickers. It didn't mean anything to him, but he decided to remember his face.

It had rained for the last four nights, and the trail was muddy enough to leave a deep rut as the wagons passed by but not too muddy to impede their progress. Charles decided that caution was necessary, and he knew he could track this group easily with this kind of trail, so he returned to his cottage to prepare for his trip on the morrow. The trip that day for the group from New hope was uneventful.

CHAPTER 13

ON THE SECOND day, the teams split. They had rearranged the wagons putting Dr. Carr's supplies in one and the construction crews in the other. The construction crew received most of the food for which Steve and Fritz were glad, as Dr. Carr's group could get supplied in the village, and the construction crew needed to spend their time working, not hunting. Calvin went with Dr. Carr's group and would meet up with Jason and Richanda six days later at the fork in the road. Again, the teams split up with the promise of improved weather ahead and no concern of anyone following. Twenty-four hours later, Charles arrived at the fork in the road and cursed his caution. Both trails could be easily followed for days to come, so reluctantly, Charles flipped his good luck but an antiquated silver dollar and chose the left path.

Two days later, he arrived at a small village in time to see Calvin and John putting up Dr. Carr's pavilion. Some of the locals were helping, and Charles faded into the background to watch and learn. By process of elimination, he was able to figure out who had gone in the other wagon and that he had chosen the wrong path! He consoled himself that he would leave at first light tomorrow to find the tangible evidence he needed.

He was engrossed in his thoughts and plans and didn't notice Calvin stopping to take a drink with a local, but Calvin noticed him and, this time, started thinking. It was all he could do to contain himself until the evening meal in the privacy of the wagon. Calvin had watched Charles go into the pub where he knew he would be for a while, and therefore it would be safe to talk. After Dr. Carr returned thanks for the food and safe travel, he blurted his news.

"Diana, we were followed here by someone from our village. I don't know who he is; I just know he watches us, and he followed us here."

"Calvin, are you sure it's not just your eager imagination taking your responsibilities too seriously?" queried John passing a knowing look toward Diana.

"No, Mr. Wells, this is not my imagination. This man in the pub is really from our village." Calvin was adapting well to his new role, working closely with adults and being free with first names except for John, his English teacher. To Calvin, John would always be Mr. Wells.

Diana intervened, hoping to provide a solution that would save face for Calvin but not encourage his evident imagination. "John, why don't you go to the pub and see what you can see. But, Calvin, you are too young to hang around pubs, so stay put."

Calvin knew she was appeasing him, but he had learned well from Jason not to let emotion overrule a cool head. He nodded his agreement and finished dinner in silence. As Calvin feared, John saw no one he recognized, and the next day Calvin saddled up to keep his rendezvous. Diana cautioned him to be careful, but he knew, in reality, they were glad to be rid of his imagination. After all, people from their own village were not the trouble over which they were concerned.

On the way out of town, he stopped at the pub to fill his flask with wine for the trip. The young girl tending the bar was about his age, so he thought he would try to pump her for information.

"Do you get many strangers passing through here?" Calvin ventured as she filled his flask.

"No, sir, your group is the first and the other man who left at first light." She timidly replied. She was obviously mind-warped and timid around strangers. Calvin choose his following words cautiously, not wishing to cause suspicion.

"Where was this stranger headed? Maybe we will meet and travel together as I don't relish the trip alone."

"He headed south down the road you came up, and he was in a bloody hurry. I don't think you will catch him."

"Maria," A voice from above called. "Get up here and start cleaning the dishes."

Calvin thanked her for the wine and pondered his next move as he mounted Ginger. This man obviously did not know the whereabouts of the other team and was retracing his steps. Calvin also knew that this first village was directly west and a little south of the construction site, and if he headed cross country due east and a little south, he should intercept Jason and Richanda before they arrived at the fork in the road. Sending a prayer upward just in case Dr. Carr was right about divine providence, Calvin galloped off, hoping his plan worked. Dr. Carr preaching his first sermon also sent a prayer up because, despite Diana and John's lack of faith, he trusted Calvin and so committed him to God for protection.

Calvin was following what had been a turnpike in years past, which wound through the mountains in the direction he wanted. The macadam was long gone, but the road was still broad and flat so Ginger could make good time. The time he and Jason had spent exploring was now put to good use as this road was well known. Stopping for only the briefest of rests, Calvin pushed on through the night, caring for Ginger's needs but neglecting his own, not wishing to waste time. At dawn, he came across the road he knew they would travel down; he could still see the tread marks in the now dry dirt path. He hoped he had judged right but was too exhausted to travel further. After tending to Ginger, he laid himself under a tree across the path and prayed Gregory did not trample him. He had judged well, and it was not until noon that Jason and Richanda discovered him.

Richanda had seen him first and reacted with all her nursing skills as she quickly dismounted from her horse to his rescue. "Jason, look! It's Calvin. Does he look hurt? Bring my bag." By this time, she was shaking a tired, dehydrated young man. Calvin came to quickly with the shaking and the cool water Jason poured over his head.

"Jason Richanda, I wasn't too late! Thank Dr. Carr's God." Blurted Calvin.

"No, Calvin, you are not late. In fact, you are early and in the wrong spot. I thought we had agreed that you would not come directly to the construction site just in case you were followed. You had better explain your actions." Responded Jason evenly but with concern. He thought he had correctly judged Calvin and his maturity level, but maybe he was wrong.

"I'll be glad to explain." Calvin tentatively responded. "But promise me you will really listen." They both sat down and nodded. "About two weeks ago at the berry pick, I saw this man leave the stream as Jason, and I arrived with the wagons. He had been fishing. Only he didn't have any fish. I didn't think too much of it at the time. The day we left for the crusade, the same man stood under a tree by the road, watching us leave. He hadn't helped us pack, nor is he a member of the congregation, but he was watching us. Two days ago, while we were setting up the tent, I saw him again, just watching. I tried to tell Diana and Mr. Wells, but they didn't believe me. Mr. Wells couldn't find him in the pub, but then he wasn't really sure who he was looking for. And the girl in the tavern said he had left at first light back down the path probably to pick up the other trail which is easy to find." As he pointed to the dry rut. "So, I cut across and rode all night to warn you. Please believe me." The last was said through a sob as Calvin burst into uncontrollable tears. The physical and emotional drain, as well as dehydration, were too much for him. Richanda tried to calm him down while Jason paced. This was not a problem Jason had anticipated!

CHAPTER 14

AFTER CALVIN HAD a fresh drink and food and with the knowledge that his friends believed him, he felt better and was able to compose himself. He was embarrassed over his loss of self-control, but Richanda assured him it was expected considering what he had been through, and she was proud of all he had done. Richanda's approval had always been important to Calvin. Of all the women in the castle, she was the most like the little bit he remembered of his mother and felt the closest to her. In fact, for a while, he dreamed that his father would fall in love with her, and she would become his stepmother, but his father was too busy playing doctor to notice Richanda as anything more than just a co-worker.

"Now, Calvin, we have a problem," Jason murmured, coming out of his musings. "What do we do with our mystery man? Do you know his name?"

"No, Jason, I never really saw him until the day of the berry pick. I never did hang around the village much, too much chance of saying the wrong thing, so unless a person were in Dr. Carr's congregation, I wouldn't know if they were part of our village or not." Calvin replied with a serious frown on his face.

That young man will change when we get back." Jason said with a smile. "If you're going to be any good to me, you need to mingle with the crowds and know everything that is going on. But back to the current problem, Richanda, any suggestions on how to deal with our friend?"

"I don't want to make this decision on my own, so if we could somehow intercept him and take him back to the castle, we can give the problem to Scott to solve. The question is how to get him to go back with us without making obvious our reasons."

They were all silent for a while until, suddenly, Calvin's face lit up with an obvious idea. "Jason, do you still have that rattlesnake rattle I gave you on your belt?"

"Yes," Jason responded and shook the rattle to demonstrate. "But I'm not sure what you're getting at."

"Well," Calvin continued, "If we rattled it at just the right point, his horse would bolt and throw him. Even if he weren't hurt, he still would not have a horse, and you and Richanda could ride along and rescue him and take him back with you."

Jason cast a sidelong glance at Richanda to gauge her opinion but could not read her. "That's a brilliant idea, Calvin. But, Richanda, how does that sit with your healer's pledge to help humanity?"

"I admit." she began slowly and deliberately. "That I do not like the potential of causing harm to anyone, but I also realize that he does not mean us overwhelming good, so I agree."

The plan was set, and Richanda rode back to tell the construction crew they would be gone longer than anticipated and to radio Scott with the plan as they were not carrying a radio. She would return to this spot and wait with the horses. Calvin and Jason started off on foot just to the side of the road, keeping in the bush. They didn't speak, using only hand signals as they slowly traveled along the trail, looking for their subject and good ambush spots. Finally, from a high vantage point, just after dusk, they saw a campfire at the top of the next mountain. They had just passed an excellent ambush site with many rocks where snakes would bask in the sun.

Calvin was to wait there with the rattle just in case Jason did not return in time, and Jason returned for Richanda. The moon had been full two nights ago and still gave good light on this clear night. He made good time as he now followed the trail and was not practicing stealth. He arrived at the meeting point around two AM to find Richanda asleep in the moss with the three horses tethered and well cared for. Jason grabbed his blanket from his saddle to form a pillow, as no covering was needed on this warm night. He told his inner clock to wake him before dawn and went to sleep.

He awoke not to his inner alarm but to Richanda frying the last of their fresh eggs. It was still dark, but as he arose, he realized he had not eaten since they had found Calvin. Richanda smiled sweetly as he woke and threw him a warm wet cloth to freshen up with.

"I assume you left Calvin in a safe vantage point and with sufficient food." She said with raised eyebrows.

"Of course," Jason responded with a look of being wounded by a dart. "I would never let the boy be in danger. The stranger is a good five-hour journey away at the top of the next mountain, and we are only two to three hours by horse from Calvin. What did Scott say when you radioed him?"

Richanda dished out the eggs while she responded. "Scott and Cindy are going to meet us north of the village, Cindy will hit him with the tranq gun, and we will detain him in a cave we have supplied up there to find out what he is up to. Scott was not pleased and hopes this does not mean we must scrap the northern branch."

"I hope not. So much work has already gone into this plan, but we cannot put the already established community at risk."

They finished breakfast in silence and were traveling toward Calvin just as the sun started to rise. Within the anticipated three hours, they had met up with a well-concealed Calvin.

Richanda and the horses were safely settled, and they again headed on foot to find their prey. Charles had gotten up at dawn and was again pushing his horse to travel as quickly as possible so he would not lose the trail. This section of the trail was rocky with occasional forks, and twice he thought he had lost the trail but found it again. Nevertheless, his haste was good for Jason's plan as a weary horse was more likely to bolt.

Jason and Calvin had gone down the trail a bit, and from a well-concealed vantage point, Calvin finally spotted Charles in the binoculars and confirmed his identity to Jason. With the identity confirmed, Calvin returned to Richanda's waiting place and Jason to the ambush site. Waiting was challenging, and once his leg cramped up, he must remember to eat a banana when this was all over, but just as the cramp was worked out, he heard Charles cursing as he rode along.

This rocky area was not his favorite for following the trail. He jerked his horse to a stop to dismount and assure he was still on the right trail. Jason could not believe his good fortune as Charles swung his leg over his horse's rump to dismount. Jason used his rattle. The result was perfect. The already tired horse bolted, and with Charles, in a half dismount, he was thrown onto the rocks. The horse headed south and was never seen again by Charles, finding for himself a much better life in a small farming village. Jason observed as Charles did not move but was still breathing and headed back to Calvin and Richanda.

As planned, Calvin crept up to the vantage point on foot, and Richanda and Jason waited a full hour to begin down the trail. Charles had come to on his own, but when he tried to get up, a wave of nausea told him to stay in place for the time being. He pulled himself into a shady spot and cursed quietly as he drifted in and out of consciousness. Two hours after his fall, he heard horse hoofs and opened his eyes to see two horses headed his way. At first, he thought it was his horse returning, and he was seeing double, but he soon realized his horse was mounted.

"Jason, look!" Shouted Richanda as she pointed to Charles. "Another traveler on this desolate road. Hello there, well, met stranger."

A normal enough greeting on the road, and Charles tried to rise to return the greeting. In getting up, though, the nausea produced results, and the open bleeding wound on the back of his head was now visible to the two who were dismounting.

"Jason, he's hurt. Get my kit." Richanda knew her lines well. "Sir, I'm versed in the healing arts. What happened to you? Were you attacked? Lay down, Jason, get some water and clean clothes." Richanda skillfully returned Charles to a supine position away from his vomit but still in the shade as she spoke. She had placed a cool cloth across his eyes and was cleaning his wound with his head turned to the side. "The wound is bad. I must return you to the castle for stitches. I'm from the Order of the New Hope. We are about two to three days' journey away, and you must have medical attention. How did this happen?"

Charles was overwhelmed by his accident and apparent rescue. These were the people he was pursuing, and he wasn't sure how to respond. He had his wits about him, though enough to realize that considerable time had passed from the time of his fall till his rescue, and her concern seemed genuine enough. He didn't think many of the Order knew him, but he felt some degree of honesty was best, so he responded.

"My name is Charles McAllister, and I know you. I live in your village. I was on a hunting trip." With the cool cloth still over his eyes, he could not see Jason and Richanda exchange glances as if to acknowledge they knew what he had been hunting for. "There was a rattlesnake on the rocks, and my horse bolted, leaving me like this."

"Well, Charles, it is fortunate for you we are headed back to the protectorate for more supplies," Jason responded with a hint of concern in his voice. "We are part of an evangelical team, but we split off to visit our northern branch. Sister Richanda, don't you think we should return to the northern branch as it's closer and our friend Charles does not look good?"

Richanda paused for a moment as if to think, although their dialogue had been well rehearsed. "No, Jason, your idea has merit, but they do not have the medical supplies needed to care for Charles adequately. He won't be able to ride, so dig into your bag of tricks and make him a litter while I clean the wound to prevent infection. And for heaven's sake, make sure there are no snakes around. You know how I hate them." She gave Charles a cup of water. "Just rinse and spit; do not swallow, or you will be sick again."

Charles was grateful for her ministrations and was too confused to think straight, so he relaxed and let these two care for his needs. He would have time to plot later.

CHAPTER 15

IT TOOK JASON until early evening to make up a litter, but they decided to progress anyway as the summer nights were still light enough to travel till reasonably late. Jason had outdone himself by lashing branches together to form a litter that was attached to Gregory's saddle, and Jason walked behind carrying the other end. He cursed the fact that Charles had a head injury because Richanda was so fearful that he would endure unnecessary bumps. Charles seemingly slept until they made camp for the night. While gathering wood for the fire, Jason met with Calvin to plan the next move. Calvin had tracked the trio after retrieving Ginger while staying unobserved. Things were taking a toll, though, and he looked exhausted.

"Calvin," Jason said in a whisper. "I want you to ride ahead and check out our path. Any signs of trouble, get back to us immediately." Calvin nodded his understanding. Jason started to draw a map in the dirt. "We will plan to camp the night here. That will put us a full day's journey from the meeting cave. I'll meet with you when I go to get wood and water." Again, Calvin nodded his understanding. "And for Richanda's sake, get a good night's sleep." Calvin grinned as Jason tussled his hair, able at that moment to let go of his current responsibilities and be an adolescent with no cares, if only for a moment.

Jason gave him a nod to send him on his way and smiled, pleased with how Calvin was adapting to the rapid changes in his life. However, when he returned with wood for the fire, Richanda looked worried.

"Jason, we must get an early start tomorrow and push hard. Even though I cleaned his wound as best I could, I think an infection is already setting in. He has a bad concussion and will need intravenous fluids to keep him hydrated in this heat. We don't know how long he was out or how long the wound was exposed to sources of infection, and then there is the concern of tetanus."

This was not part of the act, and Jason responded accordingly. "I understand your concern, but the clouds are hiding the moon tonight, and it's unsafe to travel without light. So we will leave at first light tomorrow. So now you get some sleep, and I'll care for our friend's needs."

Richanda shot him a pained look of worry but then complied, giving him a peck on the forehead as she made one last check on her patient before falling asleep by the fire.

As he sat by the fire, Jason pondered if it would not be simpler to just snuff the life out of this poor pathetic man. After all, he had done it so often during his time in the service. But what would his new friends say? It was certainly not the churchy thing to do. So he just kept watch of the ill Charles as he moaned in the night.

For Jason and Richanda, the trip the next day was long, grueling, and uneventful. Charles spiked a fever in the early morning and slept most of the trip. Spurred by Richanda's worry, they made camp only four to five hours travel from the cave. Calvin could not be found, but this did not worry Jason because he was not at the right place either.

Charles's condition had worsened over the day, and it was decided that Jason would ride through the night to the cave to get help and proper medical supplies. So, while Richanda watched the delirious Charles, Jason headed for the cave to intercept Scott and Cindy and readjust their plans.

CHAPTER 16

CALVIN HAD WAITED until the trio left before starting out. He headed due west to travel along the mountain slope until he could well pass them and then hit the trail to scout ahead. What he didn't expect to see in the early morning mist, and it was going to be a hot steamy summer day, was smoke rising from a fire halfway up the mountain. He decided it should be investigated and headed up.

The smoke was coming from a fire in the clearing just outside the mouth of a small cave. From a discrete vantage point, Calvin was surprised to see a young girl and two small boys. All three looked like they had been through a war and were struggling to keep the fire going with wet green sticks. The girl's age was hard to discern, but she looked his contemporary. She was painfully thin and had a terrified look in her eyes. Her long blond hair was matted, as it had been days since a bath. The boys looked seven or eight and were probably twins, although not identical.

After watching the trio for a few moments, Calvin decided to intervene and save the fire. He boldly walked into the clearing with dry tinder and small sticks. "Here, I think this will help your fire." He said with a warm and sincere smile.

He was not prepared for the reception his generous offer received. The boys who were innocently playing bolted for the cave, and the girl reached for a rifle he had not seen and was now cursing his poor judgment. Calvin immediately dropped the wood and raised his hands in the air, thinking that he felt like he was in a bad western.

"Sorry, I didn't mean to scare you." He stammered. "I saw your smoke and thought you might need some help."

At that, the girl looked to the sky to see the smoke rising and fell to her knees, crying. The boys rushed to her aid, throwing sticks and small stones at Calvin. Calvin quickly retrieved the rifle, set it down well away from them, and tried to reassure them of his peaceful intentions.

"Honest, I'm not going to hurt you, but you look like you need help."

The girl looked up with a tear-stained face, which caused muddy rivers to flow down her dirty cheeks. Then, through sobs, she replied. "You mean you're not a mercenary?"

"No, of course not. I'm from a protectorate south of here called the New Hope." The boys stopped searching for ammunition, for which Calvin was grateful, and the girl looked like she might smile. Encouraged, he continued. "My name is Calvin Barnes. My dad is a doctor at the protectorate, and I really would like to help." Calvin was learning tricks from Jason and put on the most innocent and sincere face he could.

The girl got up and extended her hand, still sobbing a bit. "I'm Rachel Fields, and these are my two brothers, Mark and Luke, and we need your help. Can you take us to your protectorate? They may be looking for us, and I forgot about the smoke. Can we leave now?"

This was not what Calvin expected, but he nodded and whistled for Ginger. "My horse can carry your brothers and supplies, and we can leave as soon as you are ready. Are the people after you nearby?"

"I don't know. I will explain on the way. Mark, Luke, get your things."

It took only a few moments for them to gather up their few possessions: A baseball, bat and glove, a basket of needlework, a large patchwork quilt, and of course, the gun. Calvin loaded the supplies and boys on a cooperative Ginger and fed the fire with plenty of dry wood. "So, when they find it, they will not know when you left." He explained as Rachel looked on in confusion. She nodded and followed as he led Ginger down the slope over a rocky area and down to the stream that wound through the valley. They followed the stream walking in the middle for over a mile as Rachel told her story.

"We lived with our parents on the other side of the mountain in a home alone. We were not part of a village or protectorate, although our father told us about them. In fact, he mentioned yours and said it would always be safe to go there." She looked at Calvin as if to question if she really was safe. He nodded for her to continue. "We lived off the land and didn't bother anyone. I've lost track of my days, but about a week ago, mom sent the boys out to play ball and sent me to watch. We were on the other side of a little hill, but it was cut off visually from the house. I suddenly heard our dog barking loudly and excitedly, so I sent the boys to a safe hiding place and went to investigate." Rachel had been speaking calmly and rationally, but as she continued, her voice cracked and filled with emotion as she poured out her grief. "I found a group of mercenaries standing in a circle around my mother. They gang raped her in front of my father and killed her. They could get no information out of him and killed him too."

At this point, she was sobbing uncontrollably, and Calvin put his arm around her shoulder, not daring to ask what information they had been after. She had been speaking in a whisper, and the boys did not notice her tears, being fascinated with their apparent first horse ride. Finally, she composed herself and continued.

"I heard the leader tell the men to search the house for children, so I knew I had only a short time to act. So I gathered the boys and headed for our cave. We had taken a picnic lunch with us; as usual, mom packed too much, so we have been living off that and berries. Mark felled a squirrel with his slingshot, so I was trying to build a fire to cook it, but as you can see, I failed. The boys know our parents are dead, but I think they are blocking it out."

Calvin was stunned by her story. It was evident that something was missing in her tale, but now was not the time to ask further. They were too good at hiding to be a typical family, but he would leave that to Scott. In the meantime, even Calvin knew they were malnourished and ill. Much longer on their own, and the mercenaries would have had nothing to find. And since when do girls go on a picnic with a rifle? This was undoubtedly a strange set of circumstances. He hoped Jason would forgive him for desertion but felt he needed to get Rachel and her brothers to safety. They continued at a rapid pace fore going conversation for energy. Calvin fed them from his supplies and prayed they were not followed. After two brief rest stops for Ginger's sake by nightfall, they returned to the trail and stopped to bed down only two and a half miles in front of Jason and Richanda. Despite exhaustion, Calvin kept watch as they slept.

CHAPTER 17

The last person Jason expected to see on the trail in front of him was Calvin, and certainly not with company, but it was a happy reunion. Calvin quickly explained the day's events, and Jason congratulated him on his good judgment. Rachel and her brothers slept soundly while Calvin and Jason discussed their future.

"Jason, they need medical help badly, and I know there is more to her story." Calvin proclaimed proud of his deductions. "When you meet up with Scott, send a team to pick us up too and send plenty of food. I don't think we were followed. I think the mercenaries lost interest. They usually are lazy, but she is petrified, and I want her safe in the castle as soon as possible."

Had he heard himself, Calvin would have been surprised to realize how concerned and protective he had already become of Rachel and her brothers. Jason noticed but let it drop. The boy was maturing fast.

"Don't worry, Calvin, I'll send plenty of help. We will make this a rescue mission so big it will keep the village gossips at the well busy for the next month. So you sit tight, and I'll be back by dawn."

Jason mounted and was off as fast as Gregory would go in the half moonlight. As he rode, confident of Gregory's skill, he pondered the recent chain of events. How such a simple plan could become so complicated, he did not know. Nevertheless, the original plan was scrapped, and he was already formulating a new one that he could briefly outline to Scott and Cindy, who were waiting at the cave.

"Jason, what a tangle you have bought us," Scott stated as he absorbed Jason's plan. "I must admit, though, it sure looks like young Calvin is doing a splendid job. I will personally speak with Diana and John over their misjudgment."

"Thanks, Scott. I think Calvin needs all the encouragement he can get now. I think he both needs and deserves a rest. Is there someone else we can send to fill in Dr. Carr's group?"

Cindy responded to Jason's query. "I think Harvey would love to go if he could make a detour to the construction site on the way home. It's all he talks about anymore."

Scott nodded. "Yes, I think that's a good plan. Cindy ride back, round up a rescue team with plenty of food, and add some oats for the horses. Jason and I will confer some more to firm up plans for when you return. Have Tim come from medical, I think Su Lynn is in the middle of a delivery. And bring my wife; those children may need to be mothered. And let's make this as public as possible without going overboard. Tell Sandra-Jean I want her out by the well with the women at first light so she can set the gossip straight. Jason and Richanda went to visit up north and found Charles on the way back to Dr. Carr's, and Calvin found the children while riding to meet up with Jason and Richanda to let them know where Dr. Carr was."

Cindy had a very logical mind and was already ticking off all the points in her head and would not miss one instruction. She threw Scott a mock salute and winked at Jason as she turned to leave.

Instead of further discussion, though, Jason grabbed some much-needed sleep, and it was Scott's turn to ponder, only this time without the aid of his fish. Had they bitten off more than they could chew, or had the group just become complacent over the past years, thinking the acute danger past? This was defiantly a lesson to take to heart. They must proceed carefully. He was not willing to risk anyone in the community, nor was he sure he could make the sacrifice Adam Lane had for the greater good. But, on the other hand, did he have the right to ask his people to risk their lives for a chance to shape the future? There were times when the burden of authority was more than even his massive shoulders could bear.

CHAPTER 18

JASON'S NAP WAS brief as Cindy returned with the rescue team within three hours. It was still dark out, but they pressed on. As the trail to both Calvin and Richanda was well known to everyone, Jason rode quickly ahead to make his planned rendezvous with Calvin. True to his word, the sun was just peaking over the horizon as Jason pulled Gregory to a halt in front of a surprisingly alert Calvin. Together they built up the fire; Jason whipped out his fry pan and started cooking some bacon and eggs for his hungry group. The aroma of the food woke Rachel and her brothers, and although initially fearful of Jason, with Calvin's reassurances, they simply gulped their food and listened to Jason's instructions.

"Well, Rachel, Mark, Luke," Jason said softly as he looked at each one. "You defiantly found a good guardian angel in my friend Calvin." He slapped him on the back and looked down with pride. "Richanda, a Sister of the Order, and I were also rescuing someone who was hurt on the trail, and I rode ahead to get proper care finding Calvin on the way. Please don't be alarmed but a group of seven people is coming with a wagon and horses to take you back to the castle where you will be safe. We have a hospital to take care of you; after you are better, we will discuss your future. Is that OK with you three?"

He knew Rachel was around Calvin's age, but she was so terrified and in shock that he knew he needed to speak to her like a child. Mark and Luke huddled close, having finished off seconds and working on thirds.

"I think so, Mr. Jason. I just want my brothers well cared for." Was Rachel's tentative reply.

At that moment, Tim, who was not the best of equestrians, rode up, announcing that the wagon was not far behind. He gave the children a quick check-over and looked over at Calvin with a nod of approval for a well-done job. To Calvin, that was worth it all to know his father was proud.

"Jason." Tim started as he finished checking over Mark. "The children are in desperate need of help, but I can't do anything till they get back to the castle. Can we ride on and check out Mr. McAllister and maybe bring him to this point?"

"A fine idea, Tim. I've been concerned about leaving Richanda for so long. Calvin can manage things till the team arrives." Jason responded with a nod toward Calvin, who confidently returned the nod of agreement.

They had no sooner disappeared when the wagon appeared on the trail, and soon Rachel, her brothers, and Calvin were being mothered by Frances, questioned by Scott, and cleaned up by a practical Cindy. Paul Welsh and Michael Alden rode on ahead to see if they could help Tim and Jason, while James Farrell turned the wagon around to make the return trip. Within three hours, the team returned with a delirious Charles McAllister.

Tim had started an IV and was already pumping in antibiotics. He praised Richanda for her excellent job but was already planning surgery to open up the wound and clean it. Charles was placed in the wagon, as was Rachel, with Frances by her side. To bring his wife along was the best thing Scott could have done as Rachel wept continuously in his wife's arms. The boys still seemed not to notice her tears and played with Ginger, who they now loved. Scott knew the psychological wounds were deep, and he was grateful he had done a residency in Child Psychology.

    They started back and arrived shortly after the noon meal, from which Jenny had saved plenty for the team. Rachel and the boys were moved into the private room on the men's floor, with Charles going straight to surgery. Calvin, Richanda, and Jason knew that all was well and no decisions would be made until tomorrow, so they wolfed down their food and slept through to the next day. After receiving a map from Jason and Calvin, Harvey went on his way to update the group with Dr. Carr. Scott just retired to his study to watch the fish, think and pray.

CHAPTER 19

BREAKFAST THE NEXT day was in shifts, the usual time for most people, and a much later almost brunch for Jason, Calvin, and Richanda. Tim joined them with a cup of coffee while they ate.

"Son," Tim said as he looked across the table at Calvin. "I'm real proud of the way you handled yourself recently, and I know your mother would be proud too." Tim's smile was broad, and his eyes were almost misty as he gazed at his son.

Calvin suddenly looked very sheepish and embarrassed but felt warm and good inside.

"I can certainly second that thought," Jason said as he gave Calvin's shoulder a squeeze. "But Tim, tell us how Charles and the Fields children are doing?"

"Well, again, Richanda, I can not praise your work enough." Richanda blushed but smiled at the praise. "In surgery, we found the source of the infection, a sliver of rock covered with moss was embedded deep in the wound. We almost missed it, but Su Lynn is so tenacious and thorough she found it. He will be laid up for at least a month, and we may be able to prolong that if Scott needs us to. Don't worry, Richanda, I'm still a healer." Tim reacted to Richanda's surprised glance. "We can just use some drugs to prolong the effects of the concussion to justify a longer stay with us."

"I have to admit, Tim." Richanda ventured. "I'm not too happy with our new role and would prefer minimizing the harm to others."

Jason jumped in. "Just remember my mercy-filled friend that he was after us."

"I know, I know, but it still vexes me. Is what we're doing even right? Each time we try to make a move toward our goal, we endanger lives, this time, our supposed advisory but is even that right?"

Richanda's eyes, which are so expressive, pleaded with Jason for an answer to what had obviously been troubling her. However, Jason never got a chance to answer as with eggs quickly swallowed, Calvin, replied.

"I think it's worth it for my future and my children's future. This cycle will continue if we don't work now to guide future technology. Mr. Wells always says in social studies class that we must learn from our mistakes. Unfortunately, I don't remember enough to change the future, but you do, so you must help all the children who will create the future and me."

Calvin looked both mature and innocent as he made his passionate plea to the three adults sitting around the table. They were silent as they absorbed his words. Finally, Scott, standing behind Calvin and having heard the whole exchange, broke the reflective mood.

"Thank you, Calvin, for reminding us all of what we are working towards. Are you sure you are not destined to follow in Dr. Carr's shoes? You have a lot of preacher blood in you. In fact, would you like to fill in for me on Sunday? I did a lousy job last week." Everyone laughed, knowing how Scott hated to preach, and the mood around the table lightened up. "Now, Tim, fill me in on the Fields children. When can I meet with them?"

"Scott, I know I'm the medical doctor trying to tell the seasoned psychologist what to do but tread softly with these children." Scott nodded as he sat down with his coffee." Physically they will be better in less than a week. I've treated them for the parasites they collected drinking the water, and, in a few days, the nutritional damage will be reversed, maybe longer for the girl, she starved herself to keep her brothers eating, but the mental pain will take longer and may never heal. You were right, Calvin. There is more to her story, but we daren't seek it out yet."

"Can I visit them?" Queried Calvin.

"Yes, of course, it would be good just let them lead the conversation. You have proven good discernment; she needs a friend." Tim paused a moment. "Scott, we can't keep them in medical forever, and I don't think dorm life is right yet. Any suggestions?"

"Yes, I already talked to Frances," Scott responded. "When they are ready, the boys can take over Steve's room while he is away, and Rachel can share a room with Christine. How old is the girl, by the way?"

"I know she looks young, but she says she is sixteen. Her brothers are twins and seven and a half. She did say her other brother Matthew died two years ago and was two years younger than she. However, she did not say how he died, and I did not ask."

As Tim continued outlining the medical complications caused by the children's malnutrition and parasites, Calvin excused himself from the table and bounded up the stairs to medical to personally look in on his friend. Unfortunately, as he rounded the corner to her door, he nearly knocked over Starr bringing out the morning breakfast trays.

"Slow down, buddy. No one is going anywhere." Starr laughed as she steadied the tray she was carrying. "I'm glad you're here. Your damsel in distress has been asking for you ever since she woke up. But don't stay too long. She needs to rest."

Calvin gave Starr a mock salute as he nodded his assent. "Yes, Sister Esther, anything you say, Sister Esther."

He ducked in the door, just avoiding the right hook headed his way but catching the hairy eyeball she sent him as he knew she hated to be called Sister anything, let alone Esther, even though it was her given name. He was still laughing to himself as he knocked on the inside of the door to announce his arrival. Rachel and her brothers were standing by the window inspecting their new home and jumped at his knock as if startled to fear.

"I'm sorry I keep scaring you." Calvin offered as a greeting. "Dad said you were up to a visitor but not for long." The boys came running over to hug him and asked about Ginger's health and why they could not see her in the field with the other horses.

"I'm sure," Calvin replied. "That Ginger is just as tired as we are and is resting in her stall. Don't worry. Brother Paul is taking excellent care of her. And how are you?" By now, he had reached Rachel at the window, and she blushed as she gave him a very warm hug.

"That my hero of the day is to say thanks for our rescue. I feel so much better now with food and rest, and I know my brothers are safe." Rachel turned to her brothers as she directed Calvin to sit in the chair by her bed. "Boys, play in the corner with the toys Starr bought you while Calvin and I visit. Please stay awhile. It is so good to see a familiar face, although everyone has just been wonderful, especially Mr. Jason. I hope to see him to thank him."

"Now, don't go getting a crush on Jason," Calvin responded, surprised at the vehemence in his voice. "Richanda already has her eyes on him, at least I think so." He ended with a weak laugh to cover his embarrassment.

"He is too much like my father for a crush, don't worry, but I want to thank him. We really are safe now, aren't we, Calvin? There aren't any mercenaries around, are there?" Calvin thought for a moment that Rachel must have taken lessons from Richanda on how to talk with your eyes, and he knew he would only be able to tell her the complete truth if he looked her in the eyes.

"You are as safe here as anywhere. There are mercenaries just up the other side of the southern mountain range, but they rarely come to town, and you will be absorbed into the community if you like and will always be as safe as possible." He knew it was a weak reality because there was really no safe place in this new world, but he wanted her to at least feel safe for now, and by the calmer look on her face, she was relieved by his words.

Rachel continued her line of questioning to assure her brother's long-term safety. "Where will we stay? You don't think they will split us up? After all, we are all the family each other has. "

"Well, I'm sure no decisions will be made without consulting you. After all, in our Order, you are old enough to make a commitment to the Sisterhood, so you are old enough to determine what happens to you and your brothers."

"They won't make me be a nun, will they?" Rachel responded with surprise.

"No, of course not. I just said you were old enough to." Calvin responded with a laugh. "Besides Dr. Carr, the pastor of our Order must approve you first. I know that when you are better, you will move in with Dr. Scott and Sister Frances, his wife. She was the woman with you yesterday. Her daughter Christine is a bit older than you, but just don't let her push you around."

"Could she push me around?" Rachel asked quietly.

"She may try," Calvin said with much thought. "But if she does just call on your knight in shining armor, I have a few secrets over her that she would not want the whole community to know." Calvin winked at her with a conspirator's grin, and they both dissolved into easy laughter. "I should go now, or Dad won't let me in for a return engagement. Come with me out in the hall." Calvin took her by the hand and led her to the door. "If you go down that hall and turn right at the staircase, my room is the first door on the right. If you need me for anything, come and get me no matter what time of day or night."

As she nodded in the affirmative, he gave her a quick hug and bounded down the hall, turning to give her a wave as he flew down the stairs. Rachel smiled for a moment and then turned to see to her brother's needs. She knew she had a friend and an ally, but she also realized that her brothers were really her sole responsibility no matter what anyone said. She would not let her parents down.

CHAPTER 20

IT HAD BEEN two weeks since all the excitement of the rescue, and the villagers were still talking about it daily at the well, each retelling with more embellishments. Sandra-Jean did her job well, giving out only the information Scott wanted them to hear and believe while taking in much more information than the villagers would have thought they knew. It became apparent that Charles McAllister was a loner, and few people knew where he lived. Elsie Woodbe finally remembered him mentioning a house by the old windmill. She took Jason and James there to collect some personal things for Charles for when he recovered, and she was shocked to see a working ceiling fan and refrigerator run by the windmill's passive electricity. After calming Elsie down and assuring her that the devil would not get her with two church officials present, they assured her that Charles had more than likely found the house in that state and didn't know how to shut it off. Needless to say, Charles's reputation in the village went from bad to worse when Elsie spread the gossip with all the proper embellishments. To Jason, this was only the confirmation he needed that Charles was up to no good. The next staff meeting would be interesting.

The Fields children had moved in with Scott and Frances. The boys were doing too well, but Christine had trouble accepting that she had to share her small room with anyone. It did not help that Rachel was more mature than Christine, even though Christine was older. Despite her mother's death threats, Christine went out of her way to make Rachel miserable. Rachel was stoic about the affair and did not even confide her problems to Calvin. Instead, she spent considerable time with Richanda, asking all the questions she could about the healing arts. Richanda felt Rachel was an answer to prayer and spent all her spare time training her to be a first-level nurse's aide.

    Harvey had returned the night before, and Scott convened a staff meeting to be held after the evening prayer meeting. Prayer meeting was especially crowded as all the villagers, even those not in the congregation, wanted to know how Dr. Carr was and what effect having someone with technology in the village would have on them. Scott reported that Dr. Carr's crusades were going well and gave a small sermonette on the need to accept others' faults; few missed who he was referring to. At the end of the meeting, he announced that the Order would have a special prayer vigil in the private chapel. Frances, Alexandria, and Sandra-Jean walked the villagers back as they went to turn their children into bed and to make sure no one stayed behind to talk. Through the window to the back of the chapel, it appeared that all were in devout prayer, but in reality, their holographic images were praying fervently while each member of the Order was underground in the main conference room. Su Lynn was the only other not present as it was her turn in medical.

    Scott sat back and listened to the group as they wandered in, breaking off into small groups waiting for the meeting to begin. It was hard to judge their reaction to the events of the past few weeks. Some were excited and felt they were finally progressing as they should. But would Nichole still think that if some harm came to David? And would Jonathan's inability to see beyond his nose cause some future problems? It was almost good he was safe up with Sam. And these new people, what problems would they bring with them? They would begin searching for them in six weeks, but would they even make it? Again, the weight of decisions and responsibility weighed heavily on Scott's shoulders. He took the liberty of a sigh and stood to call the meeting to order. Everyone quickly found their seats and gave Scott their complete attention.

"I thank you all for your willingness to stay up late tonight. I feel it's best if as many of you as possible are involved in decisions that affect us all. First, let me acknowledge Calvin's presence. He has certainly proved his worth of the trust we gave him when he was taught the underground. In fact, in November, when he turns sixteen, I will ask Sam to make him a Brother of the Order so he can do things on a more official level for the villagers' sake. Don't worry, Calvin. It will only be a true church commitment if you and Dr. Carr agree." To Scott's pleasure, everyone nodded consent. "I would warn you, parents, that Calvin's success does not mean that all our children are to be aware of what is happening. Each case must be judged individually. I still do not trust Christine and may never, so be sure you know your child well."

Scott paused for the full effect of his words to set in and then continued. "Many of you have not yet heard the whole story of the past few weeks beyond village gossip, so I will encapsulate it and hopefully fill in the important details. At our last major staff meeting just four weeks ago, we laid out our plans to build a home for our western visitors up north, and our plans appeared to go well under the cover of Dr. Carr's evangelistic crusade. Unfortunately, someone who now appears to be a mercenary followed the group. Calvin's keen observation skills saved the day, and Jason and Richanda were able to capture him by rescuing him. So far, he is recovering slowly in medical and has given us no factual information beyond what we found in his home, which is typical mercenary use of yesterday's technology for conveyance. On that same trip, Calvin found Rachel and her brothers. I beg you to be careful with these children. Rachel is holding a secret, and we need to crack it in a good way, or we will lose them."

Paul interrupted then. "Scott, the boys seem fascinated by the horses and spend a lot of time with me at the stables. I've worked up a good relationship with them. How far should I pry?"

Scott frowned for a moment. "Keep questions broad and avoid parent-related questions. I can't figure out why they do not mourn their parents' death. The psychological wounds must be deep, but if they want to talk about anything, let them take good mental notes and keep me informed." Paul nodded, and Scott continued. "Richanda, you seem to be doing well with Rachel. Any ideas?"

Richanda looked Calvin straight in the eye as she spoke. "I don't know if there is any early romance there, but she considers Calvin her best friend." Calvin blushed. "She loves the work in the medical department, and I think that is the best place for her. Something is troubling her at home, but she will not talk about it. She does protect her brothers, and I agree that she hides a great secret; you can see it in her eyes. How to gain her trust, I'm not sure any of us can."

Scott sighed. "I'm afraid Christine is the problem at home, but I am not sure how else to deal with it. Let's think about moving Rachel into the dorm near your room Richanda. The villagers will not be returning for another six weeks, and I think she trusts us enough to be separated a bit from her brothers. Jenny, I want one table set in a corner just for three so the Fields children can always eat together. Richanda, you can talk to Rachel about the move." Richanda nodded. "Any questions thus far?" Scott queried.

Jessica's soft voice broke the silence. "What are we going to do about Charles McAllister?"

Scott's eyes filled with compassionate understanding as he responded. "I'll let Tim update us on his status, and then I'll field suggestions."

Tim stood, obviously uncomfortable with his assignment. "The infection cleared, but his head wound was deep and is healing from the inside out. We are slipping him a medical mickey in his IV every other day, so he is still dizzy and can not stand. He thinks it's the concussion. We can only keep that up for another one to two weeks, but by then, he will be so weak he will need therapy. I figure we can keep him for four to five weeks before he gets antsy."

Tim sat down, glad Richanda did not voice her distress over the mickey. James stood to gain the floor. "Scott, may I suggest that I be assigned as Charles's physical therapist. I spoke with him occasionally at the pub, and I may be able to gain his trust to learn more about his plans. After all, as an attorney politician, I know how to bend words. Now how to stop his plans, I haven't a clue."

"That's fine with me if it's OK with Tim," Scott responded, and Tim nodded in the affirmative. Scott continued. "We will decide on future actions based on what James finds out. So Harvey, why don't you give your report now."

Harvey stood and turned red, but Cindy smiled and squeezed his hand for support as he cleared his throat to start. "Well, first of all, I think we should all do more traveling and exploring cause I know I am getting castle bound, but then maybe it is the boys, but it was great traveling around. Sam Carr is halfway done his crusade and is now in the northernmost village and will work his way southeast till he is home in about three and a half weeks. He is preaching his heart out and having the time of his life. Diana and Jonathan are making the most of it, but Diana especially is sorry she missed all the excitement."

There were some snickers as all knew their original view on Calvin's suspicions, and it was a fact among the teaching staff that they would never let John live it down. Harvey continued, slightly flustered over the laughter. "The construction team is doing well. I was able to help them out for a couple of days. The underground plant is dug and framed with an access tunnel to the best house standing, and a basic castle frame is up. I think Michael needs to go up now cause it will need a lot of work with the landscaping to hide everything and make it look old. They are also running low on raw materials and really need someone to forage in the city so they can keep working." Harvey sat down there by ending his speech.

"Thank you, Harvey." Scott began. "And yes, I heard your bid to go back up, and I think it is a good idea. Since the main intrigue is happening back here, I want Jason and Richanda to stay here but take Starr with you this time to let her use her new first aid skills if needed." Starr's eyes bulged as she nodded in evident excitement. "Julie, why not let Nichole watch the children and you and Michael go on a second Honeymoon up to the Northern Order as a cover story." Julie, Michael, and Nichole nodded yes. "Good. I am sure you and Starr can help put the existing buildings in good order. Plan to leave in two days. Harvey and Starr leave tomorrow to help Dr. Carr. Plan to re-meet him on the way back, so you come home together. Frank, I know those are organ-playing fingers, and they are not used to manual labor, but I need you in the garden, or we will not have enough food for ourselves, let alone to share with our new friends."

Frank laughed softly. "No problem, Scott, just don't make it a permanent assignment, or your wife will never forgive me if I can't play for the harvest cantata."

Everyone laughed, knowing how strictly Frances ran the choir in Ron's absence. Scott bought the meeting back to order.

"Don't worry, Frank, Eric, and Ben will protect your playing ability, and think of the tan you will get. Ok, on to the next order of business. When Jason left, his group was fifteen adults and thirteen children, but that doesn't mean the group is still that small or large. Whatever size they are, I want to split them up to help them adapt and take advantage of some of the skills coming over. For instance, Jason reports a dentist on board which I know many of us will use. I want all their medical people down here to learn how to set up a non-technical hospital: five people, two doctors, two nurses, and the dentist. They also have a theological student who I am sure Sam would like to train, so I need six volunteers to live north for the winter and help our friends settle in. It may be rugged living conditions. Any volunteers before I start picking."

Ben and Helena raised their hands immediately, and Scott looked at them with a twinkle in his eye. "Any ulterior motives there, Ben and Helena?"

"Of course not," Ben grumbled. "Helena can help set up shop, and I can get the garden going. Totally innocent on our part."

"OK, OK." Scott laughed. "But I doubt there will be much to garden this winter. Two down four to go any others up to the challenge or opportunity?"

Tim ventured. "You might want to ask Su Lynn. She's been complaining of lack of inspiration for her poetry, and she could see to the medical needs while their people are down here."

James then broke in. "If things work out with Charles, I'll be glad to go and take my daughters with me. They may even find a husband in the new group, so I guess you could put me in the opportunity group. But, of course, Sharon would pine away for Steve, but maybe he could come too."

"Suggestion is well taken; James and I will talk to my son when he returns. He may have found he likes it there. But three children, even though adults by today's standards, don't count towards the six. In fact, I'm asking my two oldest and Paul's kids to move up and start the village. They all know what is at stake but choose to live the simple safer village life rather than put on the charade. I would feel good knowing they were there to help establish the area.

Eric jumped in. "Well, if you are sending Ruth Welsh up, I might as well go up with Fritz, or he will never forgive me." Everyone laughed as Fritz's crush on Ruth was well known.

"I see that hand, Harvey." Chuckled Scott. "But no, I think I'll ask Ron to stay up there and leave it at that. I need you here with the boys, and what would Cindy say about moving right after the wedding? After all, Eric, you, and Ron came from the north, right?" Scott smiled at his irony, and Eric chuckled.

Scott continued. "After we have found our friends and settled them in, we will bring them all down for a house raising for Nichole and David." At that, Nichole beamed and restrained herself from giving Scott the hug he deserved. "That way, in the mass confusion, we can get to know one another without the villagers suspecting too much. They will, of course, stay for the wedding, and it will seem like mutual consent when our groups split up and re-assign. For now, assignments are temporary, but if you want to stay north, we can discuss it. Any questions?"

Of course, there were lots of questions, and the prayer meeting went into the wee hours of the morning to discuss all the details, but the group as a whole left via the chapel, pleased with their plans and praying the westerners arrived. For once, Calvin left with much on his mind as he pondered his new role in the scheme of things and his feelings for Rachel, who he both wanted to protect as a friend, and yet he knew that he might be needed to help discover her secret. There were aspects of becoming an adult he did not like at all.

CHAPTER 21

EVEN IN THE natural seclusion of the valley, news travels fast especially bad news. And so it was that the next day a man who made his living traveling from village to village fixing pots and performing other odd tasks for food or goods left to head north with his horse and pack mule. As he enjoyed the summer day, he was unaware of the crucial part he was to play in the lives of others. Near noon of the second day, he approached the mountain where the Fields had lived. He usually stopped at the Fields' home, but from what he had heard in the village, there was no sense in doing that now. It was too bad cause Mrs. Fields always had a sweet smile and a carrot or two for his horse. In fact, he figured he was the only person who had known they lived up there.

Martin Fields had always looked forward to news from around the area, and the news he had always earned him a night's rest, food, and shelter for himself and his animals. The next village was a challenging four days journey by this route, and the Fields house was a nice place to rest before pressing on, too bad. Ray did work for the mercenaries when asked to but never went out of his way to find them. He was glad the Fields' children were well cared for. On his next trip, he would stop and see them.

He was surprised to come out of his musings and see that his horse, and he guessed he himself was stuck in a habit, and they were heading up the trail to the now vacant home. Well,

Ray thought it was worth a look to see if the mercenaries left anything behind. Margaret, he had named his horse after his wife, whinnied loudly, but no smiling face appeared. Ray tethered the animals in the stable and entered the home through the doorway with the door swinging on only one hinge. It had been ransacked first by humans and then by the squirrels, raccoons, and mice. In the half-light of dusk, he looked around and found a lantern with some kerosene and lit it. Ray found a travel sack and started filling it with blankets that were not ripped, which were only a few, some toys he knew were unique to the boys, Rachel's handwork kit and some items her mom had made, clothing, and all the pictures he could find. That sack was for the children, and he would ensure they got it. Then he filled another sack with pots, pans, candles, tools, and anything else he thought he could trade along the way. He was unsure why he did it, but he placed the children's sack in a closet, found a warm corner, and went to sleep.

His sleep was short-lived as he was rudely awakened by a bright light on his face and cold, sharp steel against his throat. Standing over top of him with his hands on his hips was Glenn Casey. He spoke with authority as one who was used to getting his way. "Well, old man, you look like you could use a shave, and Nick here would be glad to oblige, but if you fail to give me good answers, his fingers may slip."

The threat was not lost on Ray, and the fear in his voice was evident. "Whatever you want is yours. I'm just the local tinker. I have even done work for you, but we never met. My horse and mule with the tools of my trade are outside. I don't work for precious metals or jewels, so I've none to give you."

Glenn laughed. "That much tinkerer Ray I know. What I want is information. What brings you to this house?"

Ray had collected his wits and decided that the truth was his best option, but he would watch his words. "I usually stop here for the night on my route between the New Hope and High Point protectorates. It's kind of halfway, and the Fields who used to live here usually put me up, and I fix a pot or two. The Mrs. gives Margaret a carrot, and old Sally the mule gets fresh oats, and I play with the kids. I came here tonight and found this mess. Looks like they have been gone for weeks, and the place is trashed, so I availed myself of a place to sleep and, to my shame, pilfered some usable wares to barter with along the way. It will be a long winter; the more goods I have, the better I eat. If I may be so bold, what are you doing here?"

Ray knew the question could bring on an angry retribution, but he also knew that men who were not curious usually had something to hide, and somehow he wanted to protect the knowledge he had of the Fields' children. For all he knew, it may have been Casey's gang who killed the parents.

"You may ask if you please," Casey replied and signaled for Nick to let Ray sit up without the knife decorating his throat. Ray could not even have thought of escape as the room was filled with men, and the doors were blocked. "We found the place as you did, and even though we Mercenaries have a bad reputation, we like to police our own area, so we were waiting for the culprits to return. The parents are dead. We buried them out back but whoever killed them took the children. Mrs. Fields' diary mentions you frequently, so we know you are not involved cause you would have avoided the house on the way to High Point since it's not the most direct route. So since the folks are dead and we have plenty of supplies, we will let you pilfer. Your sacks have been checked. It would behoove you, though, to mention this to no one. After all, we still want to punish the scum who did this to these nice people."

Casey's voice became almost co-conspiratorial, and Ray did not trust him. He had lived a long time through his wits, and his facial expression matched surprise and disgust at the right moments. Casey bought his story hook, line, and sinker, but Ray's mind still raced as Casey continued. "You say you just came from New Hope?" Ray nodded. "I hear there was some excitement over a rescue, but no one seems to have much information. Can you help?"

Again, Ray thought that truth was the best plan but not too much of it. "The townspeople won't tell you much 'cause they are a superstitious lot and are afraid the devil will invade their village. Oh, about two weeks ago, Sister Richanda and Brother Jason found a man on the trail. His horse had thrown him and cracked open his head. It seems he is pretty bad off, and they had to send a wagon to bring him back. He's been in the hospital since, and a few days ago, the Brothers went with Elsie Woodbe to his home to collect some personal things and discovered electricity working some high-tech devices. Well, Elsie is still blessing herself. I have a feeling that Charles McAllister will be run out of town when he recovers unless the Brotherhood takes him in." Ray chuckled over the last part of his narrative, hoping it sounded natural, but he was rewarded by Glenn's reaction to Charles's name. "Anyway, that's why they won't talk, afraid the television will curse the village."

Someone from the back yelled. "Sounds like the kind of trouble that lazy Chuck would get into. I say we leave him be and let him come crawling back to us. Then he will be grateful to do the dishes." Everyone laughed, only it wasn't pleasant.

Casey paused as if weighing his words and motioned for the room to clear, and it did immediately, except for Nick. "Old man, it is hard to threaten one as old as you with death as you are too old to care, but if I discover that you have lied to me, I will make sure your death is slow and painful." Nick's grin enforced Casey's words. "Spend the night here. You will be safe as my men are all over the mountain. Tomorrow you can continue your route; as I said, you are welcome to your sack. It's less for the raccoons to play with. I have men in every village, so I will know if you are spreading words about this incident, and I would not like that!"

Ray nodded appropriately and looked appropriately scared, which he was. Glenn Casey was wise because Ray did not fear death, he was prepared to meet his maker, but he wanted to do it in bed asleep. After a moment to let his words sink in, Casey continued. "Good night, old man. We will watch you leave tomorrow. I would not come back here again if I were you."

And suddenly, the room was black, and Ray was alone. He lay back in his corner but could not sleep. He hoped he had done well and somehow protected the children. He had watched them check his sack out of the corner of his eye, and they never found the children's sack. Knowing that even Casey's men could not see in the dark, he, by touch, rearranged his sack, placing smaller pots in bigger pots, and was able to consolidate the two sacks into one. It looked a little bigger, but maybe they couldn't tell from a distance. He would separate things again in the next village. Just before dawn, exhaustion took over, and he slept until the sun hit him in the eye through the window. He tended to Margaret and Sally, whose packs had also been inspected and saddled up, apologizing to Sally for the extra load, and headed northwest to High Point. He would follow his regular route, but if he cut out the three most northern villages, he could be back at New Hope in three to four weeks, and Casey would not be the wiser.

And in fact, after the third village Casey gave up following the old man considering him a red herring. In Casey's mind, Charles McAllister was the least of his concerns, and the date of the rescue was a full eight days after their raid. The children could not have survived on their own that long someone had found them and was hiding them, and he was determined to find out who. So he drew his attention west, leaving a small group to watch the house. Only the girl could unlock the secret of Mrs. Fields' diary, and Casey had to know it!

CHAPTER 22

Life at the castle seemed to calm down into a routine. The villagers did not seem to care that so many of the Order were traveling this summer or that the hunting team rarely came to town and never with much meat. They, too, had summer concerns like planting, caring for animals, preparing for winter, and caring for all the babies that popped in June and July. Word via the transmitter from the construction crew indicated that all was well, and Dr. Carr's group had stopped en route to the easternmost village on their trip. Scott was pleased and started to make plans for the arrival of the western group when disaster hit.

As the village expanded, the local enterprise expanded, and five village men banded together to form a logging operation to produce the raw materials needed to facilitate this expansion. It was, of course, a primitive operation with handsaws and the use of pack animals. It had rained heavily the night before, and the ground supporting a pile of logs had eroded. No one had inspected the supports that morning, and as Jack Brady and his son Philip were milling the timber at the base of the hill, Ed Moore and Zack Black were loading more timber on the pile on the slope.

The mill consisted of a raised stilt platform on which the log was on top. One person stood underneath with the two-person saw, and one man walked on top and working together, they were able to mill the logs. It may not have been the most efficient setup, but it worked until someone rediscovered even a water-powered sawmill. Zack was standing in front of the log pile as Ed rolled a log in place. Unfortunately, the impact was all that was needed, and the logs broke loose. Even though Zack jumped to the side, both legs were crushed. Jack Brady was also crushed, but the supports for the mill spared his life by stopping the full impact. Philip was thrown from the top and knocked unconscious, his arm and collarbone also crushed.

It took all day for the rescue team to get them off the mountain. Once at the castle, the entire medical team spent the next thirty-six hours trying to save Phillip's life and put the other two back together again. Phillip's fiancé, Mary, was hysterical, and Tim heavily sedated her and placed her and her mother in one of the girl's dorm rooms. Amazingly enough, the women's ward was empty, so Tim and Su Lynn turned it into a trauma unit. Strict visiting hours were imposed and maintained as Scott authorized the use of necessary yet dangerous equipment if it was discovered. In the back of the medical ward was an elevator leading to an underground plant. This facility was not connected to the rest of the underground plant. It was an ER's dream facility and had been built up over the years with careful pilfering of the city hospitals, which were now vacant. Jack and Zack were heavily sedated "for the pain" and transported down for complete X-Rays, while Philip was taken one floor lower for a CT scan, revealing a large, life-threatening blood clot between his brain and skull. Tim and Richanda went into immediate surgery. Scott had been trained to administer anesthesia and was used as Su Lynn worked on the other two, who were now back upstairs, unaware that they had been subjected to a technological device.

Phillips surgery was ten hours long, and despite a lack of real expertise in neurosurgery, Tim's performance would have been praised by any doctor in the field. The most frustrating part was the need to make a perfect surgery look like a crude job. Tim opted for a burr hole below his suture line, hoping the families' relief would stall questions. Philip was still deep in a coma as he was transported topside and would remain in one for some time. All three would recover, but they would require extensive care over the next three to four weeks, and it was unsure if Philip would have permanent brain damage or not.

With Starr gone and the group's resources generally depleted, Richanda decided to orient Rachel into nursing the fast way. Rachel had moved into the castle and seemed to blossom under Richanda's care. She had a natural knack for nursing and quickly picked up on what she was taught. She asked Richanda if she could wear a habit while she worked so she would be in "uniform," and Scott agreed it was a good idea.

And so, when Richanda approached her the day after the accident to request that she take over the complete care of the men's ward, Rachel rapidly agreed. There were only four patients on the ward with minor problems, and Charles McAllister's intravenous had come out the day before the accident, so Richanda was sure she could manage their basic care. Rachel was pleased to accept the responsibility and attacked her responsibility with excitement and dedication to detail. Her mother had been a nurse before the smashing and taught her much, but she had not let Richanda know that piece of information that was too dangerous. Nevertheless, she decided she would not let Richanda or her mother down.

She had returned to her normal weight in the four and a half weeks since her rescue, and her hair had returned to its natural luster and body. She wore it in long braids wrapped around her head, causing her to look like a real angel of mercy with a halo. Her green tunic highlighted her hazel eyes, and the men on the ward always brightened when she came on to perform her duties. Rachel had an incredibly tender heart for Charles. As the medical mickey wore off, he realized how weak and defenseless he was and felt alone and scared at the mercy of his supposed enemy. He hadn't remembered seeing Rachel before, but he never paid much attention to the children of the Order, so he assumed she was the daughter of someone in the Order. It did not matter; they became quick friends as Rachel always spent extra time making his bed or just sitting and exchanging light conversation in her free moments. Charles had never had anyone show him concern or kindness, so between Rachel and James Farrell's afternoon therapy sessions, he was becoming a new person. No one knew his vital role in unlocking Rachel's secret.

    A little over a week after the accident, Ray returned to the village and went about business in the usual way heading to the well at sunup. In a village with no modern conveniences, including simple plumbing, it was essential for the women of the village to gather each morning and draw the water for the day. A few houses close to the protectorate were able to rig a simple system using the force of the falls to secure basic plumbing, but most villagers thought that too scientific, and the common belief was that the women did not want to give up their gossip spot. It was understood that the protectorate should have plumbing as they were too busy doing "God's work."

    The women looked forward to Ray's trips as he bought news from the other villages and functioned as an informal long-distance mailman. And so, on this hazy August day, the women were pleasantly surprised but happy to see Ray earlier than expected. Ray mingled with the women giving them the news they sought and setting up appointments for personal home visits to show off his wears and do any needed mending. Ray was equally interested in the accident and concerned for the families affected. He made a mental note to stop by and see Mrs. Brady as she was now completely without men folk at home. Ray had a heart of gold for all his gruff exterior, and the women knew it.

Finally, he spied his target as Sandra-Jean Fitzgerald approached the well. She was a jovial person who never recovered her youthful figure after the last two children. Slightly subconscious about her chubby exterior, she compensated with an effervescent personality and was, therefore, the perfect liaison to the village people. She never wore her habit to the well, preferring to be thought a villager by passing strangers, and the women loved her dearly. She, too, was surprised to see Ray, but her mahogany brown eyes never let on. She kept her thick wavy hair cut short, and the red highlights in her light brown hair shone in the morning sun as she greeted Ray.

"Well, well, if it isn't, Ray, come to bend our ears with stories and talk us into repairs we don't need."

Ray nodded and smiled at the ongoing joke that sometimes he was given work to do to keep the storyteller around, not for real need. Then, finally, he tipped his hat and replied. "As you say, Sister Sandra-Jean, but now what would you need to be done in your home, and shall I stop by to see Sister Jenny today?"

She replied as she lowered her bucket into the well with a grin of mischief. "Oh, I don't know. I think we may have found someone else to do your job. But, of course, it depends on your price. You know we are careful with God's goods."

As she lifted the bucket, Ray intervened. "Here, let me lift that over for you, Sister." As he grabbed the bucket, he placed a wad of paper in her hand and hoped she was as surreptitious as he suspected. He was rewarded as she did not bat an eyelash and pocketed the note as he dumped the bucket into her barrel, waiting on a small cart. Ray finished drawing all the water she needed, and the other women watched, thinking Ray was trying to win over Sandra-Jean's business. As she left with her cart, he resumed marketing the other women still there and then went off to his first appointment, breakfast at the pub if he fixed the teapot. Not a bad way to start off business.

On the other hand, Sandra-Jean waited until she had deposited her load into the storage bin outside her house. She did not need the water, but she made sure it was used as long as she went to all the trouble to get it. Once safely inside her home, she investigated the paper. It was well-written, proving as Sandra-Jean had always suspected that Ray was not the uneducated fool he portrayed. However, reading the note, she became concerned that her friend may have stumbled onto a hornet's nest. The note read:

> I NEED TO SPEAK CONCERNING THE FIELDS CHILDREN BUT IN SECRET. A TRUSTED BROTHER SHOULD MEET ME AT THE FISHING CREEK UNDER THE OLD WILLOW TREE AT 1:00 TODAY.

Sandra-Jean left for breakfast with much on her mind as she ushered her children out the door.

CHAPTER 23

THE BREAKFAST CROWD was sparse this morning, and Jenny had sent the village help home early as the regular kitchen crew could manage things. Sandra-Jean was relieved to see Jason and Scott sitting together and deposited her children with Nichole as she headed for their table. Some of her usual jovial expression was gone, and Scott noticed the change immediately and rose to greet her. "Sandra-Jean, please join us. We have plenty of empty chairs." Jason also stood and picked up that the mood was serious. Sandra-Jean wasted no words.

"Scott, Jason, I'm glad I caught you. This note was passed to me this morning by Ray the tinker." She passed the note to Scott, who read it, and then he passed it to Jason as she continued. "He is back from his northern circuit earlier than usual. He looks OK, but from how he passed this note, he did not even trust talking at the well. I've known Ray for seven years. He's neither mind warped nor a mercenary or high tech. I think he just likes the simple life he leads but would also support us. However, I feel someone needs to keep this appointment."

Having said her piece knowing her job was done, she started eating her breakfast as Scott and Jason debated. "Jason, what do you think of this?" Scott queried.

Jason lightly tapped his fingers together, stalling for time, and finally, with a puzzled look, responded. "I don't know, Scott. I've only met Ray once in passing, but I trust Sandra-Jeans judgment on his character and motives. Maybe he stumbled on to something in the mountains on his trip. He was here in the village at the time of the rescue. Do you want me to meet him?"

Scott also stalled in his response and with a now familiar sigh. "Yes, Jason, I want you to go fishing for dinner. Only take Calvin with you. Ray may not trust you as a newcomer, but he trusts Calvin and knows him well, and the two of you are known to go fishing on occasion. Sandra-Jean, you did well, as always. If you have occasion to speak to Rachel today, drop the fact that Ray is here and let me know her reaction." Sandra-Jean nodded as Scott continued, "I do not have to tell you to use caution, Jason, and don't clue in Calvin beforehand. Let his responses be perfectly natural. Also, Sandra-Jean spread the word to track Rachel in case she is spooked by Ray being here." Both nodded in agreement, and Scott rose to go to his office and think.

Right after lunch, Calvin was thrilled to have Jason invite him on a fishing trip as he had not seen much of his hero recently. Ray watched from under the tree as the two fishermen approached the stream with his pole already in the water. He had already caught two good-sized trout, which he planned to give to the Brady's for dinner. He did not know what to expect, but the newest Brother with Calvin was unexpected. But then again, if Brother Scott had gone fishing, it would have looked funny. Well, he could be discreet and would play a word game with them if needed. As Calvin and Jason crossed the wooden bridge, Calvin spied Ray, although Jason had found him much earlier, waving called to him.

"Hey Ray, how was your trip? Are you taking a vacation already, or will you trade fish for dinner tonight?"

Ray laughed and relaxed a bit as Calvin was a good friend. "No, young Calvin, this is for Mrs. Brady. My heart goes out to her and the family. How are her men folk doing?"

By this time, Jason and Calvin had reached the tree, and Ray stood to greet them.

"Dad is taking good care of them. Philip came out of the coma last night but is really confused and will need a lot of care. Ray, you remember Brother Jason, who joined us from the Northern branch last spring?"

"I sure do greetings, Brother Jason. This scamp been bothering you much?"

Jason laughed as he returned the firm handshake. "No, not at all, Ray, I kind of like having Calvin around. Do you mind if we join you fishing, it looks like a good spot from your catch thus far? Sister Jenny wants trout for dinner, and we do not want to disappoint her."

With a sweep of his hand in the general direction of the tree, Ray indicated they all should sit. No one said much as hooks were baited and lines cast, but once all was settled, a casual conversation began. At first, they talked about the crops expected this fall and the accident, and Ray's trip. Then, after a sufficient amount of lighthearted talk and six fish later, Jason decided to dig for information. "Ray, I know you were here last month when Calvin found and rescued the Fields children, were you not?"

This was what Ray was waiting for, but he was still cautious in his response. "Yes, I was, sure was a sad story, but I was proud of Calvin. Never did like mercenaries."

Before Jason had a chance to continue, Calvin jumped in with an enthusiastic question which Jason felt could not have been better planned. "Hey Ray, I never thought before, but you travel up near where I think their home was. Did you know them?"

Ray nodded slowly in the affirmative. "Yes, Calvin, I did. I stopped there every time I went to High Point Protectorate. Mrs. Fields was a real fine woman and her husband a good friend. The children call me Uncle Ray." Ray's voice was noticeably sorrowful, and Calvin held his response, waiting for the mood to clear. This time it was Jason who jumped in on the conversation.

"It must have been a shock to you then. I know it can be hard to find those you trust," Jason emphasized the word trust. "But maybe you could help us help the children."

Ray paused, sizing up Jason's response and judging if he should talk in front of Calvin. Finally, Jason realized his dilemma and responded. "Don't worry, Ray; Calvin did not know about your note, but he also can be fully trusted. I've been watching, except for some fish; we are completely alone."

The surprised look on Calvin's face told Ray that Jason's words were true, so he poured out his whole story of how he knew the Fields, how he stumbled back to their home, how he collected various goods, and all about Glenn Casey's visit. He left out no detail and ended with the fact that the bag for the children was in the last stall of the protectorate barn.

Jason was pensive for a moment taking in all the information. Calvin was also introspective, realizing for the first time how much danger his friend was in and that her fearful behavior was well grounded. Ray just waited for someone to speak, and finally, Jason broke the silence.

"You were wise in all your responses to this Glenn Casey, and it is interesting to note Charles's involvement with him. I think it's best, Ray, if when you leave here, you do the Southern circuit skipping Slippery Creek Protectorate as it is Casey's home turf and then plan to winter here, and we will gladly put you up at the castle, I feel it would be safest for you." Ray nodded as Jason continued. "What concerns me is why Glenn is still interested in the children and what is in the diary that motivated him to read it so well as to know about you. So many questions need to be answered, and we must think carefully about how to produce answers. You should avoid seeing the children just in case you are still being watched. The children are perfectly safe, and Rachel rarely leaves the medical wing these days. What did you say was in the sack you bought for the kids?"

"Toys, a sewing kit, some blankets, some handmade things from Mrs. Fields, and many family pictures." Ray mentally ticked off his list. "They didn't leave much intact."

Jason thought a moment longer and started gathering his equipment to leave as he issued instructions. "Ray, finish fishing and continue your business in town as normal. I believe you go to the well daily?" Ray nodded. "Good. I think passing more notes is potentially dangerous so if you see Sandra-Jean with a yellow bow in her hair, come fishing. Otherwise, stay away from the protectorate. I will have Jenny at the well tomorrow to inform you of the general lack of work. Then, Calvin, I will head for the barn to retrieve the sack, and you drop off the fish and tell Scott to meet me in his office."

Jason rose and shook Ray's hand, and they were off. Ray sat back and pondered the conversation and realized that Brother Jason was OK in his book. He was also thrilled he had not let the whereabouts of the Fields children slip. An hour later, he was headed back to the village with five fish for the Brady's and not a care in the world.

CHAPTER 24

SCOTT AND JASON arrived at the underground office simultaneously; only Calvin was not present.

"Where's Calvin?" Questioned Jason with a puzzled look. "I would have thought he would want to be here?"

"I'm not sure." Responded Scott. "He told me you needed to see me but then mumbled something about adult business and ran off. I think that boy has wisdom beyond his years, but I wonder if we are pushing him too fast. I'm on pins and needles. Jason, fill me in."

Jason re-told Ray's story, and Scott drank in every word interjecting questions when needed for clarification. Finally, when completed, Scott let out a long slow whistle. "Those children needed more rescuing than we thought. So what's in the sack?"

"Let's find out," Jason responded as he emptied it onto the table. The blankets were quickly placed to one side, and the toys were quickly dispatched. Scott glanced at the one big family picture and passed it to Jason to see if it meant anything to him. Jason's response was unexpected. "Martin Fielding, I cannot believe it's him. No wonder Rachel is scared."

The picture had meant nothing to Scott, but the name was all too familiar. "Jason, are you sure it's Martin Fielding? I thought he died before the war broke out?" Scott responded with a look of surprise.

Jason's voice became almost computer-like as he relayed to Scott all he knew. "Yes, Scott, I'm sure. Remember, I was hot on the trail of things through the service. Martin Fielding is the device's creator, although we never believed he meant it to be used the way it was. He was reported killed in a car accident, and his family disappeared after the funeral. Helena will know him well. I believe you said she was on your team looking for a cure, and he was the secret to it. To think a group of senseless mercenaries ended his life. What do you think they wanted then, and what do they want with the children now?"

"I don't know, Jason, but I don't think we can let Rachel keep her secret forever. I, too, would like to see Mrs. Fields' diary. What a simple changing of the name to throw people off."

Just then, Sandra-Jean rushed in, looking very worried. "Scott, I did what you said and saw Rachel in the hall. I asked if any bedpans needed mending as Ray was in town. The poor girl looked at me in terror and ran for her room. I thought you should know right away."

Jason and Scott looked at one another and bolted for the door. Scott yelled over his shoulder to a stunned Sandra-Jean. "Her dad was Martin Fielding." Sandra-Jean took in all the ramifications of that statement in a split second and also bolted for the elevator.

Rachel had been on her way to medical when Sandra-Jean had stopped to talk. As much as she loved Uncle Ray, his presence in the village was, as she saw it, threatening her security. If he had spread the word that she was here, her brothers might be in danger. Better he thinks they all died when next he stopped at her home. In the safety of her room, she scolded herself for revealing her feelings to Sandra-Jean. She quickly packed some essentials and ran out the door. She planned to raid the kitchen, quickly collect her brothers, and head for the hills, but her dedication to her patients held her back. After all, no one knew she was running away, and Charles needed to be out of bed for the evening meal; if she did not do it, it would not happen. She deposited her load in a corner and walked into Charles's room.

He was waiting for her as usual but quickly noted that all was not well. She assisted him out of bed to the chair by the window and turned to leave. As she started to leave, Charles did something he had never done before. He reached out with compassion to someone else and said. "Please don't go come here and tell me what's wrong."

Rachel started to cry as she turned and looked out the window, not at Charles, and replied. "I must leave, Mr. McAllister; a group of mercenaries killed my parents. No one knew me here, so I was safe, but someone who does know me had just arrived. I'm sorry I will not be able to see you get well, but I must protect my brothers from Glenn Casey. It may already be too late."

It was Charles's turn to break down and cry, which he did profusely while holding Rachel's hand tightly. Rachel was confused and scared as she tried to comfort him. "It's OK, Mr. McAllister. My brothers and I will be OK on our own. I have learned much from Calvin about living in the woods. But, I really do have to go." She pleaded as he clung to her hand.

Between sobs, he replied. "No, Rachel, you do not understand. You must forgive me before you leave, or I will never forgive myself. I am a mercenary, and I work for Glenn Casey. When I had my accident, I was trying to prove these people were high techs. I was to have been a part of the raid on your house, but I felt my scheme to overthrow the protectorate more important. I was thinking of living the life of leisure, not in the people who would be affected."

Rachel was shocked out of her crying and stood with her mouth open in front of Charles. He had let go of her hand and was openly sobbing. Even though Charles was related to the group that had killed her parents, he was also her friend, and she knew he had changed. She put her arm across his shoulder, hugged him, and softly said. "I forgive you, but I still have to go."

No one had heard Calvin enter, but he gingerly put his hand on Rachel's shoulder and whispered. "No, you don't. You are safe here."

Rachel looked into his eyes in both disbelief and hope and saw Scott, Jason, and Sandra-Jean run into the room. It was too much for Rachel, and she fainted. Charles looked scared, not knowing how much Calvin had heard, and Scott was surprised to hear a very mature Calvin turn to Charles and say. "Don't worry, Mr. McAllister, you are as safe as you always were. We are a religious Order, not mercenaries who rape and murder."

Scott and Jason had a million questions, but Sandra-Jean had already revived Rachel, freeing her from Calvin's arms, and recruited Jason to take her to Richanda's room to be checked. She sent Scott to get Tim and Richanda and permitted Calvin to stay with Rachel, as she knew that was all he would do anyway. Michael Alden was just then delivering the meals, and he was firmly told to keep Charles company until relieved.

Charles was suddenly left alone with Michael, who knew nothing of the events of the day, so Charles had time to reflect and worry about his friend. In Richanda's room, Rachel was revived and looked up to a room full of concerned faces. She felt trapped and safe at the same time. Calvin was the first to speak.

"Rachel, just because Ray knows you, it is no reason to run. If anything, he is trying to protect you and, in fact, risked his life already to keep your secret, and we can protect you better than anyone. Just tell us why you need it."

Before Rachel could answer, Scott intervened. "Calvin is right. Ray does care for you more than you realize and further risked his life to bring you some things from home, Including some family pictures, so we already know your name is Rachel

Fielding, and we know of your father's involvement with the device. We do not understand why Glenn Casey is putting so much energy into finding you."

Tim and Richanda reacted to the name with an audible gasp, and Calvin looked confused. Tim then intervened as Rachel broke into tears. "I am sorry, Scott. No more answers now. Rachel needs to recover from the shock. Richanda get her a sedative and have Sandra-Jean stay with her. Everyone else, including you, Calvin, clear the room."

Tim spoke with authority, and everyone scampered, although Scott lingered to study Rachel a moment. Then, in the hallway, he announced that the meeting would reconvene in Jason's office in five minutes and sent Calvin to get James up from dinner to be present. Not for the last time, Scott pondered the weight of responsibility he carried and the lives entrusted to him. It would be a long night.

CHAPTER 25

JAMES HAD A mouthful of beef when Calvin tapped him on the shoulder and whispered that he should join him in Jason's room. Despite the lack of villagers at the moment, Calvin decided that discretion was best. Without question, James followed him up the staircase, giving credit to Calvin's status as equal to any adult in the community, and the two walked silently into Jason's room. The office was too small for the group, so Scott had moved the two chairs into Jason's room. Jason's double bed took up a large part of the room, but a low chest was along one wall at a right angle to the bed, and Tim and James sat on it. Scott placed the two chairs, so a circle was formed, one for himself and one for Richanda, leaving the bed for Jason and Calvin. Scott wasted no words as soon as James and Calvin were seated.

"Calvin explain to me what just happened and how you came to be on the scene?"

Although Scott was not angry at Calvin, the tension in his voice was evident, and a sensitive Calvin timidly replied, gaining confidence as heads nodded in encouragement. "After I gave you the message from Jason, I decided it would be more important for me to look after Rachel. After all, I had heard Ray say to Jason it sounded like Rachel was not safe with mercenaries, and I didn't like her taking care of Mr. McAllister, so I went to my room, and with my mirror exactly right, I can see who comes up the staircase. I saw Rachel come up for her dinner duties as expected, but I also saw her hide her travel sack, and she looked scared. She did not see me follow her, and when she went into the room, I went to the supply closet cause if you peek between the second and third shelves, there is a hole to spy into the room. I overheard everything and went to stop her from running away, and you all came bursting in on the scene."

"Excellent, Calvin. I'm glad you were there. Now, exactly what did you hear?" Scott queried, this time keeping the tension out of his voice. Calvin related the conversation almost word perfect, and the room was silent as the adults absorbed it all. Finally, Scott spoke, filling James, Tim, and Richanda in on Ray's discoveries and the findings in the family portrait. When he was done, Richanda and Tim looked shocked, Calvin confused, and James just let out a long low whistle. Again, the room was silent as minds worked to assimilate it all. This time James broke the silence.

"Scott, where does this put us with Charles? Rachel has obviously impacted him, but how far do we trust him?"

"Actually, James," Scott replied. "That's why you are a part of this meeting. I'm trusting your skill to glean from Charles that information tonight. I want him on a twenty-four-hour watch, even closer than a suicide watch. Tim set up four-hour shifts. Every male in the community just volunteered except Calvin. And make sure someone is always within shouting distance." Tim and James nodded. "On a more delicate nature, how do we handle Rachel? Calvin put yourself in Rachel's shoes. What are you feeling now?"

Calvin thought for a moment and replied. "That's hard, Dr. Scott because I would have punched Charles McAllister out, but she hugged him. I am defiantly confused myself, so I guess she is. I know protecting her brothers is her top priority, so that I would keep them together for now. But, I do not think she should be alone either."

Scott nodded at Calvin and glanced sideways at Richanda. "How about a women's opinion on the topic?"

Richanda never even took the time to breathe as she had been formulating her plan before Scott even asked. "It is now obvious that Rachel Fields or Fielding is mature beyond her years but under considerable stress. I agree with Calvin that she needs to know her brothers are safe, but I think she needs rest too. So tomorrow, she should sit in on a meeting just like this one, only below. She needs to know we are high-tech enough to help her, and she needs to take charge of the decisions that affect her life. I also think she should continue caring for Charles as soon as she is up to it. I did not think he had anything worth redeeming, but she proved that wrong tonight, and no offense to James, but I think she is the secret to winning over Charles."

Tim and Jason nodded in agreement as Scott pondered. "OK, Richanda, we will move the boys into the dorm room across from your office, and I will move a cot into your room for tonight. It will be best if she sleeps in your room tonight, as we can get her below without being missed. James, you get the first watch with Charles and Jason; you have midnight to four, so go grab some sleep as soon as we vacate because I want you at the meeting with Rachel. Calvin do whatever feels best. You continue to show good judgment. I also want you at the morning meeting. Any questions? No, good meeting adjourned. I'll go get the boys, and Tim can move furniture." Everyone left to their assigned tasks.

James was unsure how to approach Charles, but he entered with a small smile as he relieved Michael, who was still very puzzled. Charles had been gotten back into bed but was propped into a sitting position. James took a seat beside him and broke the tension-filled silence.

"Well, friend Charles, it seems you triggered some excitement today. Do you want to talk about it?"

Charles looked genuinely concerned as he responded. "Please just tell me, is Rachel going to be all right? You won't hurt her, will you?"

James looked as if he had been wounded as he replied harsher than he would have liked. "For heaven's sake, Charles, we are here to protect her, not rape her mom and kill her folks." James had not meant to be so biting, but he was still shocked over the manner of the Fields' death, the fact that it had been planned, and the fact that Rachel had observed it all. Charles openly sobbed.

"Brother James, this may be hard to believe, but I never meant that much harm to come to anyone. The bottom line is I am lazy, and I thought by hooking up with the mercenary's life would be easier, only it wasn't, so I left the camp, and Glenn told me if I was his eyes and ears in the village, he would take care of me. He kept his side of the bargain, and I kept mine, but the men in his group looked for ways to taunt me. Soon Casey started verbally abusing me, calling me the scum of the earth, so I started to believe it. Then when I overheard two of the Sisters talking on the berry pick last month, I thought I had found a way to overthrow Casey and gain the respect of the men. I planned to follow your group to gain evidence that you were high techs. A few days before Dr. Carr's group left, one of Casey's men came to get me to help in the raid of the Fields place. Casey had been watching it for over a year. If I had not been on my own search, I would have gone and been a part of that slaughter. I am not sure I can forgive myself. Can you forgive me for what I planned to do to your group?"

Charles had stopped crying but was pleading for forgiveness in his voice and eyes. He was undoubtedly a desperate man. James cleared his throat and searched for words. He was not a believer in Dr. Carr's religion, although at times he wished he were, and this was one of those times. "You will have to talk to Dr. Carr about how to find forgiveness for yourself, but yes, I forgive you. It is obvious that Rachel already does, and yes, she will be fine, a little shaken up but fine. If she is up to it tomorrow, she will come to see you. For now, though one of the Brotherhood will stay with you at all times, I'm sure you understand."

Charles nodded silently and laid back and at least faked sleep. James was not sure. The conversation had been enlightening, but it did not help him decide if Charles could be trusted. And if he could be trusted, how far? There were indeed many questions to be pondered.

Jason was prompt for his shift, through which Charles slept while Jason pondered and schemed. He thought back to his days in the service and thought of all the ways of eliminating a problem. Unfortunately, all of them meant permanent harm to Charles. He should have taken care of Charles on the trail and been done with him. He knew Richanda would disapprove if he eliminated Charles. In fact, she seemed more distant since the rescue. If things calmed down, he would have to work on winning her over. After all, it had been a long time since the death of his wife. And he was ready for a new wife.

On the other hand, the object of his thoughts did not sleep well, waking every time Rachel turned, worrying again over the outcome of the meeting the next day. She was not sure her idea was good, but she also believed they could no longer decide Rachel's destiny. Why was it so hard to save the world from themselves? She sent many prayers heavenward.

Tim was up all-night caring for Philip, who took a turn for the worse but rallied just before dawn. Scott spent the night with his fishes, so the next morning only Calvin and Rachel woke up refreshed for the day.

CHAPTER 26

RACHEL WOKE ALERT and refreshed as the sun poked its first rays through the mountains. In the gray of dawn, she could make out the cot Richanda was sleeping in and instantly remembered the previous night's events. So many emotions swept through her mind in a moment. Her hero Calvin was there for her again. Her friend Charles was part of the gang who killed her parents, yet she knew he had changed, so she felt betrayed and worried for her friend. And then there were the concerned yet compassionate faces of Richanda, Scott, and Jason. Maybe it was time to trust someone. Despite her courage and fortitude, the strain of protecting her brothers was becoming too much, and as she lay quietly in the bed, tears flowed to release the pent-up emotion.

When Richanda got up to check on her, she noticed the tears and wet pillow but said nothing about them, glad she had found release. Instead, she smiled softly as she clued Rachel in on what was to come. "I know events last night were quite a shock to you. I hope you slept well?" (Rachel nodded in the affirmative). "Good. You are going to be treated to breakfast in bed with your brothers who slept across the hall last night." (Rachel's eyes lit up at that, but she still kept quiet) "We told them you were coming down with the flu, so they are not overly worried and are unaware of last night. We really do want to help and protect you, sweetie."

Richanda brushed back a wisp of Rachel's hair just like her mom had done on so many occasions, and Rachel burst into tears as Richanda hugged her and gently rubbed her back. As the tears were being dried, Sandra-Jean popped her head in with a basin of warm water. "I thought you would like to freshen up before I escort your brothers in. To say the least, they are excited about breakfast in bed."

The tender moment was broken, and Richanda watched as Rachel lost her vulnerable innocence for a mature adult attitude as she prepared to continue protecting her brothers. Richanda sighed, thinking how devastating the device was to spoil the best years of a young girl's life. As the last braid was tucked, Calvin appeared with Mark and Luke and joined them for breakfast. Rachel was glad for his company as he kept her brothers distracted from asking too many questions, and she felt secure with a friend who had remained so faithful. Once the meal was done, and Jenny had outdone herself to make it memorable, Calvin ushered the boys out, saying that Rachel needed her sleep and if they hurried, they may convince Brother Paul to take them on a trail ride. He saw them safely down the staircase and returned to the now-alone Rachel. She greeted him with a hug and smile as he entered the room again.

"Calvin, I have no idea what will happen, but I know you are a good and faithful friend. Thank you."

The tears were gone, but her voice still had a quiver proving they were still close at hand. Calvin led her to sit on the bed again as he explained what would happen next. "Rachel, what I said last night was true, we do want to protect you, but we need to know why we need to. I'm going to take you someplace that is top secret, but we want you to understand that we have the capability to protect you. Is that OK with you?"

Rachel squeezed his hand and nodded in the affirmative. Calvin left her on the bed while he crossed the room and activated the elevator. He watched her response as the door opened. It was one of surprise, not horror, as she walked over and stepped in without encouragement. Then, as the door closed, Calvin gave her an oral history of the castle.

"Our group has been together to a certain extent for the last eight to ten years. First, we built the underground plant while we were trying to track down the cause of the problem. Then when the smashing occurred, we built the castle and moved here to form the religious Order. I, of course, did not know any of that until about two years ago. The religious Order is our cover, and not everyone believes in Dr. Carr's religion, but those who do the vows they take really mean something."

At this point, Rachel looked Calvin in the eye and asked quite seriously. "Are you a believer in Dr. Carr's religion?"

Calvin frowned and replied honestly. "I really do not know. I guess I'm still deciding. I prayed a lot on the trip I found you, but I am not sure my prayers made a difference. I don't know if faith is all facts in your head about God or if it's emotion or both. I know I plan to talk to Dr. Carr when he returns."

Satisfied with his answer, she let Calvin lead her out of the open elevator door as they arrived at their floor. As they walked down the hall, Calvin let Rachel peek in the rooms as he continued his tour.

"We have many rooms filled with all the art we could safely transport. The forage teams are still finding stuff. Our computers hold the world's knowledge, and we have at least one prototype of every major electrical gadget you could think of. Basically, what my dad and the others are doing is helping assure you, and I have a good future that is not deprived of the benefits of technology or destroyed by it. The villagers trust us completely, especially after Mr. Lane's death. Someday I will tell you the story but trust me when I say that Glenn Casey does not dare show his face in the village. His men rarely come in, but we can protect you no matter what."

They had reached Scott's office, and Rachel instinctively knew she would be facing others but not sure who. Calvin squeezed her hand and sent her a smile as he concluded his monologue and opened the door. "And now, Rachel, some concerned friends want to talk with you."

Scott had raised the wall thinking the fish would be a positive influence, and he was correct. For a moment, Rachel just stood in awe of the fish swimming along one whole wall of the room. Richanda, Jason, James, Scott, and Tim were seated in a circle with three empty chairs. Scott motioned for the two newcomers to sit and started the meeting.

"Rachel, I'm glad you're looking well. Sandra-Jean will be joining us momentarily with some refreshments. It may be a long morning. I hope Calvin gave you a good tour?"

Rachel's voice was hesitant but not fearful. "Yes, Dr. Scott, dad always said we could trust you, but I didn't know this much."

Scott smiled, knowing Rachel's emotions were taut. "Rachel, I know last night was difficult for you, and I wish there were another way, but to help you and your brothers, we need to know your whole story, and I beg you to hold nothing back as the more we know, the more we can help."

Rachel looked around the room and could read the care and compassion in each face. She took a deep breath and began her narrative. "As you already know, my name is Rachel Marie Fielding. I was seven years old when my dad "died" in the car accident, so I remembered our old name, but as you suspect, mom and dad planned the accident to disappear and start a new life. Matthew never questioned the shorter name, and I was responsible enough to remember. At first, we moved around a lot, and dad would disappear for extended periods of time. Finally, just at the smashing, we moved into our home. I learned later that dad had been working on the house for years and all the moves were to throw people off, and when he was gone, it was to work on the house."

"It too has an underground plant but not near as extensive as this one. My father never meant to use the device as it was used, and he spent the last ten years of his life trying to undo the damage. Finally, he developed a device to counteract his original at the time of use but could not reverse the mind damage already done. Uncle Ray was about the only other person we ever saw."

"The twins were born a year after we settled in, and we were a happy family. Dad was always a person who would be moody, especially when he would finish an unsuccessful attempt at his experiments, but he loved us dearly and spent a lot of time with us. However, my father made one error in judgment about two years ago. Dad decided that a trip to a village market would be fun for the whole family. We were self-sufficient on our farm, but once in a while, one of them would forage in the cities. This, though, was a trip to a village with people. It was fun, and we had a memorable day."

"On the trip home by horse and carriage, we ran into trouble. Glenn Casey and one of his men stopped us to demand a tariff for safe travel. Dad gave him a sack of flour and beans, but he started to make obscene remarks in mom's direction. Dad was getting ready to defend her honor, but mom held him back and softly called his name. Glenn's eyes lit up, and he called to his buddy. "I knew I recognized the face. It's Martin Fielding". Dad pulled out his pistol and shot Glenn in the shoulder and his partner in the leg, wounding his horse as well. They had not been expecting that from a farmer family, so by surprise, we were able to escape."

"Dad drove the team till they almost dropped away from home. Once we were safe, he headed north and traded the wagon for extra horses. We took a very roundabout route home and hid out, hoping Glenn would not find us. That is when I learned about the underground plant and its history. Dad taught us everything about computers and electronics as quickly as he could. The twins were only four but picked up on computers quickly. Dad said their IQs are off the charts. Unfortunately, in his zeal, dad forgot to teach us electrical safety, and Matthew touched a live wire after just washing his hands. He was killed instantly, and dad became obsessed, saying that Casey would not be the cause of his family's death. I guess he knew then that he would be found, so he started to teach us to hide and travel unseen. Unfortunately, he did not teach me to survive in the wild, just how to hide. I guess he always thought he would be around to come and rescue us."

"Last December, a mercenary rode by and asked to stay the night. It was snowing heavily, so dad could not turn him away. Now it seems he was one of Casey's men. Mom and dad became extra cautious, and dad spoke of moving again, but mom's health was poor since Matthews's death. It was then I was charged with the safety of my brothers. Only I can bring them to remember mom and dad and the underground. Only they know the code to get in; I cannot. Dad hoped this would protect us."

"The day of the raid, we were not on a picnic but escaped in the underground tunnel. After I had the twins safely in a halfway cave, I snuck back to see if I could help, but the rest of my story is true. When I returned to the cave, I told the boys, and they had a good cry, and then I put them in the innocent memory. That is why Dr. Scott they do not seem to mourn; they do not remember, and sometimes I envoy them. The cave where Calvin found us is well hidden, and for several days we stayed deep in the back and heard Casey's men looking for us. When Calvin found us, we had reached the end of our supplies and strength, and I was planning to travel that day to seek shelter in a village. I'm grateful it was Calvin who found us, not Casey."

Sandra-Jean had arrived quietly and heard most of her story while she stood behind Rachel and, at that moment, reached down and hugged her shoulders and cried. Tears were also flowing from Richanda and Calvin, who had been trying to hold them back until he saw moisture in Jason's and Scott's eyes. Again, Rachel allowed the tears to flow and knew she was safe. There were some awkward silences as everyone composed themselves. Finally, Jason broke the mood.

"Rachel, you have done very well, and I know we are all proud of you. Ray is a good friend and has already risked his life to keep Casey from finding out about you." To Rachel's look of horror, Jason quickly responded. "Don't worry. He is a wise old man and safe. We plan to make sure he stays that way. He stopped by your place and bought you some personal things but was questioned by Casey. Fortunately, we found out more information than Casey did. He is looking for you and seems really interested in your mother's diary. Can you explain why?"

Rachel looked brave and scared all in one look and responded evenly. "Brother Jason, my mother's diary holds the key to understanding what is in my father's underground plant, but only I can break it. That was how dad wanted to protect what was there. We are each part of a key but useless alone. So Casey wants me to break the key and give him the secrets of mind control."

Richanda next asked. "But honey, what does he want? How could he know what is under your home?"

"After our first encounter with Casey, dad racked his brain to figure out how he knew him, and then he remembered a junior network executive who was passed over twice for promotion. He knew enough to comprehend what dad was working on but not enough to be part of the trial. Dad had the only known working transmitter for the device. Many people tried to work with the device, but the transmitter was essential to breaking down the mechanism of function. Dad also had some mind-controlling machines, one of which is responsible for the twin's present state. I think Casey wanted to control everyone in his world. I would rather destroy our home than see him succeed."

Rachel's face and voice took on an unaccustomed hardness as her mind thought of revenge. Scott's mind was racing as he tried to think through all his options. He did not want to endanger his current operation, yet the contents of that underground plant could be vital in his hands and dangerous in Casey's. Still thinking, he queried Rachel further.

"Rachel, can we reach your underground plant by your escape tunnel?"

"Yes, it can be done but only by Mark and Luke together. But if Casey's men are watching that closely, we may not even be able to get to the tunnel."

Scott responded as he tapped his fingers together in a steeple. "I'll let Jason take care of that by setting up a diversion. I think we can use Mr. McAllister to our benefit. Tim, after lunch, I want the boys down here so Rachel can release them to mourn," Scott responded to Rachel's gasp. "Now, Rachel, they need to cry. Even with the loss of memory, the trauma will work on their subconscious. They may then choose to stay in the memory they are in, which would be a tragedy. Jason give them plenty of time to cry but eventually find out how to get into the tunnel and underground. Sandra-Jean send Ray fishing tomorrow, and Calvin meet him and tell him his southern trip is canceled. I want him to move into the castle. Jenny will produce a good story. Tim, I want you ready with a sedative, but it is time I talked with Mr. McAllister. Richanda, you oversee Rachel. Any questions? No. Good meeting adjourned."

As most of the group got up to perform their assigned tasks, Rachel sat stunned, and Calvin rushed to his friend's aid. "Dr. Scott can be abrupt when he's thinking of a plan. Dad told me it is cause he worries about everyone and feels responsible for our lives. He can take your breath away, though."

"As always, Calvin, you are the reassurance I need. Thank you." And for the first time in a long time, Rachel smiled and really believed there was hope for the future.

CHAPTER 27

THE TWINS JOINED Rachel for lunch in Richanda's room, and after the meal, Rachel broke their mind control. As their memories emerged, the two boys dissolved into tears, with Frances and Sandra-Jean there to help them cry. It was an excellent grief session. Once they were more composed and yet still weepy, Jason took them below and used the fish to continue calming them down. As the boys lost themselves in the tranquility of the fish, Jason also thought things through.

He had wanted to settle a score with Glenn Casey ever since he learned of the manner of Adam Lane's death, but now, he was even more sure that any meeting with Casey would end in a final resolution of the matter. But how to do this and keep the children safe? A plan began to form, but it was certainly risky, and was the risk worth it? A look at the still grieving but more composed Mark and Luke told him it was. Jason focused then on to the here and now.

"Mark, Luke, I know you are sad, and it's good to cry, but it's also good to get on with life and help us punish the men who did this. Are you willing to help?"

Both boys nodded in unison, and Mark let out a sniffle as Jason continued.

"Good, now draw me a map of where the tunnel is and how I can get in."

Mark jumped in. "But you can't, Brother Jason only my voice and Luke's thumbprint can open the door." Luke nodded his head rapidly in agreement.

"That's OK, boys, we can work around that. Just tell me how to get in and what has to be said."

The boys drew detailed maps and spoke the passwords into a recorder. Jason took a mold of Luke's thumb and left it for later to recreate a flesh-like thumb. Rachel put them back into innocence memory for their protection, but daily grief sessions were now planned with the boys and Sandra-Jean.

Charles McAllister certainly was a changed man, and Scott wished Sam was back to be a spiritual comfort to him. But, unfortunately, Scott could not afford that luxury if he were to gain Charles's co-operation. Charles had eaten and was returned to bed for the afternoon. Scott and Tim relieved Ben, who went to hide his frustrations in some piano playing. Despite the apparent repentance in Charles, it was all Ben could do not to end his life. Adam Lane had been a good friend, and Rachel was too young for all her sorrow. As he left, Scott saw in his eyes the look of so many he had seen in the pictures from the holocaust. Scott made a mental note to talk with Ben later. The last thing they needed was a revenge seeker. But for now, he patted his shoulder to say well done.

Tim and Scott sat on either side of Charles, with Tim ready to use the hypodermic tranquilizer if needed. Scott opened the conversation.

"Charles, you present me with a problem. I do not wish to harm you, so why should I let you go, as you have already stated ill intentions towards our religious Order? Although why you should wish to harm us, I cannot tell. Charles, give me some reason to trust you beyond the confines of this room."

Charles certainly had the look of true repentance and was so concerned now for someone else he forgot to plot and plan ahead, so for once, his answer was genuine.

"There is no reason beyond the fact that I freely admit I was trying to find evidence that you were High Techs. I never got my evidence, only suspicions. You saved my life, and Rachel saved my humanity. I had forgotten how to care for someone. I do not want to find the evidence now; I would like to work here to redeem myself. I've always been lazy, and now I see good for nothing, but I want to be someone Rachel can be proud of."

Charles's voice became hopeful as his eyes pleaded with Scott forgetting that Tim was in the room. Scott weighed his words carefully. Charles would not have known about Ray's story, but Ray's account matched Charles's self-assessment.

"Charles, we do not require manual labor as punishment. No harm was done to us. If you wish to join our Order voluntarily, you must speak with Dr. Carr to determine if you are a true believer. If he is satisfied, you are welcome to join us. The harm you have done is to Rachel, although not directly. We have learned that your associate Glenn Casey still looks for her and her brothers. We would like to do everything necessary to ensure their safety. Are you prepared to help us help them?"

Charles did not hesitate in his reply, "Brother Scott, believe me when I say I would die to save that girl from further grief."

Scott rose to indicate that his interview was at an end, parting with these words. "Let us pray it does not come to that, but we will keep in mind your offer as we make plans."

Tim stayed with a subdued Charles while Scott returned below to make plans with Jason. They conferred past dinner, and Scott was not entirely sold on Jason's plan but also saw little choice. It was a blessing that Sam was not back yet but would eventually find out. Scott prayed he would not protest too much. Before Scott could approve the plan, Richanda joined them, and Jason found an unexpected ally as he revealed his plan. Both men watched Richanda closely for her reaction.

"I admit that parts of it go against my very being, and I hate putting anyone in danger, but I also admit we seem to have no choice. How much of a risk are we putting her in?"

"Actually, very little because I will be with her all the way." Responded Jason, unable to believe that Richanda supported his plan.

She continued. "And how much can we trust this, Charles McAllister? He could blow the whole plan."

Jason sighed "I admit he is the weak link, but we will plant a bug on him to monitor his words, so we should have no surprises."

Scott joined the discussion. "I'll agree it's a plan, and I'll even face Sam's wrath, so when do we put it into action?"

Jason stood over a table map as he outlined his timetable. "We should send Charles on his way Sunday when Sam Carr is due to return. I learned from a reliable source that Casey is currently camped in this range, giving Charles time to get to him and our team to the house. If all goes well, Casey should call off his men to chase Rachel, giving us free access to the underground. I think we should only tell Rachel what she needs to know. I don't want Charles to know too much of my plan."

They all agreed, and the meeting was adjourned. Jason went to find Calvin, who was essential to the plan's success Richanda went to check on Rachel, and Scott went to the chapel to do some real praying.

CHAPTER 28

SUNDAY MORNING, JUST before dawn, Eric woke from a sound sleep to find Charles gone. He raised a quiet alarm, but Charles was not to be found, and a horse was missing from the stable. Eric just kept apologizing to everyone.

"I don't know how I fell asleep. I even drank a cup of coffee to stay awake. I couldn't have been asleep that long. He couldn't have gotten very far."

But indeed, he had, and despite a complete search, he was gone. Scott issued a general caution to the community, and Sandra-Jean dropped the right words at the well. Ray, having moved into the castle to "overhaul the kitchen plates for the new school year," told his tale of meeting Casey with all the proper embellishments. Sam's group returned and were briefed accordingly. Scott just watched his fish and prayed.

Three days later, the villagers watched, amazed, as Jason and the new girl Rachel left, heading west. Sandra-Jean said it was to find a safe hiding place, but few in the village thought it was a good idea except for maybe the stranger who had arrived that morning. She had said she was from Slippery Creek Protectorate, a four-day journey by foot south of New Hope, and was stopping for rest on her way north to High Point. She was accorded the customary hospitality given to travelers, but the village women thought it strange that a young woman should travel alone and so far. They were more amazed that she left quickly without buying supplies for the ten-day journey.

And had they stopped spreading gossip long enough to notice, they would have wondered why she headed south, not north. Sandra-Jean noticed, though, and reported to Scott.

That night with no moon in the sky, a small party slipped out of the village unseen heading north. They rode in silence and kept off the main roads. By dawn, they met with David and Ron, who had traveled down from the construction site. They erected a camouflaged tarp and slept while Ron and David kept watch, and Diana went ahead to scout out the area. At dusk, she returned to fill them in as they ate sandwiches. No campfire for this group tonight.

"We are well camouflaged, which is good" Heads nodded as all eyes were riveted to Diana. "Not as many followed after Jason as I would have hoped, but Casey did, so those left behind are more relaxed and sloppier. Our stranger appears to have been Casey's woman as she is acting in charge but does not have the hold Casey does."

Then Rachel piped in, "Any sight of Charles?"

Diana's voice was kind, although her military training prevented too much emotion. "No, honey, I didn't see him. I imagine Casey took him with him to identify you. Jason will see he is cared for."

Rachel did not like the sound of Diana's voice. She knew that her friend's escape was causing extra caution, but she still had trouble believing that after all, he had said he would still sell her out to Casey. Rachel shivered at the thought of someone she considered pure evil and could not tell if it were the cool autumn air without a fire or the thought of Casey and what he would do if he caught her. Richanda noticed the shiver and quickly moved by Rachel, encircling her in her cape and comforting her without a word being spoken.

Meanwhile, a blazing fire was going in the west, and Jason was cooking dinner. Being the bait was not his idea of fun, but the plan seemed solid. Starr was Rachel's size and hair color, and with the proper clothing, it did not take much to fool the villagers. He knew Star was safe because Casey needed her; his concern was that he was just extra baggage to be disposed of. The big question in all this was Charles. Jason had his senses sharp for any signs that they were being watched. Starr seemed relaxed, but then she was an actress, and he did not dare break their cover by questioning her as they ate.

The moon was approaching full, and tonight was not as overcast as their first night had been. Jason could clearly see the entire site as he went to tend Gregory and Starr's mount after dinner. He was surprised to return, finding Starr gone. Hoping she had simply gone to relieve herself, he called out in a normal voice. "Hey Rachel, you left the fire unattended."

The anticipated response did not come, and he called out more fervently as he looked around. He found Starr's ring that he knew she would drop only if attacked, and as he looked for a trail, he found one on the opposite side of the fire, away from the horses. The trail was not secret, so he knew Starr was fighting all the way, therefore he knew she was safe for now. Jason had thought they would take him too. This was unexpected. As he gained on the group, he could hear Starr struggling and men cursing under the load. Just as he thought he would be within sight of them, he heard a noise that sickened him in the stomach, and as he gained the clearing, he saw the jeep pull away with Casey's men and Starr. Motorized transport had not been counted on. He quickly returned to camp, finding it ransacked and the horses cut loose. His "canteen" was still there, so he radioed Scott to fill him in.

The advantage he now had was that he knew where they would take her, so he whistled for Gregory. In the distance, Jason could hear the startled reaction and thud as Gregory threw his abductor and retraced his steps to his owner. Jason wisely avoided that path but headed Gregory northeast to the Fields' home. He could never overtake the jeep, but he might arrive in time to lend a hand if things went wrong, and he and Gregory could go places the jeep could not. The growth around the mountain's base was too thick for the jeep to penetrate even if it were a 4-wheel drive vehicle, but Gregory could pick out a trail; getting to the other side may be faster than Casey could drive far enough west to circumvent the mountain. At least Scott would warn Richanda so they would be on their toes. Jason was glad for the bright moon as he picked his way through unexplored areas, hopefully in the right direction.

    Richanda, on the other hand, gently cursed the moon as she realized she must speed up the timetable and work without the cover of complete darkness. The element of surprise was still on their side. She briefed her team, and each prepared to leave in silence. Each knew their task and knew the importance of silence and surprise. David would stay behind to watch the horses; she knew she could count on Mark and Diana. Ron and Eric were unknown factors untried in actual difficulties, but their skill was so needed. She smiled as she glanced over at Calvin tucking Rachel's hair into a black cap and smearing her face with some of Starr's black grease. She thought over the changes in him in the last six months and how Rachel would not have been rescued if the New Hope Protectorate had not been preparing for the Western group's arrival. Yes, it was a good day when Jason rode out of the mountain, but even with his help, could they rescue their future? And what part would he play in her future? She enjoyed his company but could never wholly read his intentions. Were they big brother friendship or romantic love? And where did he stand with God? He was never home long enough for her to figure that out. Richanda sighed and caught herself sounding like Scott and cleared her head of distractions concentrating only on the task ahead. The group responded, and with her hand signal were off.

Keeping in the trees, Rachel led the way to the cave, which was the tunnel's eastern entrance, and cut through the small mountain between her group and her former house. Mark and Diana stood guard at the entrance while the rest proceeded in. As Rachel moved rocks in the proper sequence to reveal the elevator door, Ron admired the genius behind its construction and whispered:" If only Michael were here to see this, he could get some pointers."

Rachel smiled, glad for the compliment honoring her father, and then turned to give instruction. "Once we open this door, we must be silent. A speaker system runs the entire length and is automatically broadcast in Dad's workshop. Dad did not want to be snuck up on. Even if they have not found the underground, the noise would be heard in the house and reveal our presence. So Calvin, get us in."

Calvin placed the recorder near the speaker, and Mark's voice was heard, giving the command to open the door. At the moment requested by the LED readout, Luke's fake thumb was placed against the panel, and the door slid silently open. Eric, Ron, Richanda, and Rachel proceeded in while Calvin stayed behind, prepared to open the door again if needed.

The tunnel was a simple six-foot by six-foot square of reinforced steel, with each section wedged into place and welded in as it was dug out. It had taken Rachel's father four years to complete it working alone, but his efforts were worth it as it saved his children. Ron could walk upright at 5-9", but Eric's 6-3" frame was cramped, causing many stops to rest his back. Because of the stops, it took just over an hour to transverse the three miles. When they finally arrived, Rachel pressed some keys on the terminal built into the wall and could both determine that the workshop had not been occupied since the date she and her brothers fled, and the door silently slid open to admit her.

Once inside, she whispered to the group that whispering was now safe because she had deactivated the speaker system in the room but not the tunnel. Rachel directed Richanda to the computer terminal and used her password to open all the files. While Richanda downloaded all the files to thumb drives, Eric and Ron started loading the transportable equipment onto the dollies each had carried in. Each dolly was loaded to the max with still more valuable equipment. Backpacks were loaded with anything of value, including several DVDs Rachel's father had made explaining his theory. Finally, Rachel made room in her pack for a family portrait that included her parents and her other brother. Only Richanda saw her slip it in and cried within at the great sorrow this girl carried.

Two hours later, the group started the long trek back. Despite dismantling the speaker system, no one spoke but concentrated on hauling their load up the tunnel. It was only a five percent grade, but each one carried enough equipment to make the return journey difficult. Richanda breathed only a partial sigh of relief. There was still so much that could go wrong.

CHAPTER 29

O<small>N THE OTHER</small> hand, Starr was having the time of her life. Although her abduction had been none too gentle, the ride in the car was great. Starr had been a bit of a daredevil speeder in the days before the smashing, so it was easy to portray the thrill and enthusiasm that a sixteen-year-old Rachel would have felt along with the fear at the car careening over the dirt trail. In addition, she had seen Jason in the clearing as they pulled away, so knowing he was safe, she both enjoyed the ride and stayed alert to learn what she could.

Starr felt sorry for the driver as Casey constantly yelled at him as he tried to pick out a path on a trail no longer built for even the best 4-wheel vehicle, which this one was not. Charles was not with this group, so she was not surprised when they pulled to the side after half an hour of travel. Bound and gagged, Starr was pulled from the jeep roughly by Nick, who enjoyed his job far too much. To the man waiting in the shadows, Casey yelled. "Well, is this Rachel Fielding or not"

Charles's voice was clear as it spoke in the dark. "Yes, that is the girl who cared for me. Her name is Rachel Fields, and she has two brothers."

"She is supposed to have three. Charles, if you betray me, it will be the last thing you do." was Casey's malicious reply.

Charles stepped into the head-light of the jeep, looking like his old mean self. "I can only tell you what I know. Ask her"

Starr looked petrified as Casey approached, and it was not all an act. He ripped away her gag and yelled at her. "Well, girl? Where is your third brother?!"

When Starr did not respond, Nick roughed her up aggressively, and between sobs, she yelled. "He's dead. You killed him by forcing Dad to teach us about computers. A live wire electrocuted him. Are you satisfied?! You have killed my whole family, so just kill me!"

"Actually, my dear," Came Casey's sarcastic reply, "you still have two brothers left, and if you don't co-operate with me, I won't kill you. Instead, I'll kill them and let you live with the knowledge that you could have saved them."

Starr lunged at Casey, beating him with her bound hands while calling him every despicable name in the book. Casey only laughed while Nick quickly pulled her off of him.

"Throw her in the back. We leave now. Charles, we no longer need your services. Our new camp is just outside Slippery Creek, and Slippery Creek belongs to us, so head there and find yourself a safe cave to crawl into. I need men I can trust on this mission, not fools and weaklings."

Before Charles could respond, Casey was in the jeep, and the engines were roaring. Charles waited till they were well out of sight and started down the path to return to New Hope. He hoped the young lady was safe and wondered where Jason was, but not knowing what else to do returned to his new home.

Starr was re-gagged, which made her job easier, and she was relieved that the weakest link in the night's chain of events was now over with. All the fielding pictures were seven years old, and the night Casey found the family, Rachel had been cloaked for warmth in the back of the rig. The mercenary who had visited last winter had not been permitted to see the children, so Starr now felt safe in her identity as Rachel. Her concern now was that the time schedule was off. She may have to rescue herself unless she can slow down the jeep.

Her silent musings were answered as she heard the all too familiar sound of air escaping from a flat tire.

A very flat tire was observed as they all alighted from the jeep, and Nick dragged out Starr. On closer examination, Starr realized all the tires were almost bald, to begin with, and were not meant to survive this environment. Ed, the driver who was obviously an abused flunky like Charles with no backbone, cowered as he revealed to Casey there was no spare.

Casey's response was to knock Ed on his back and curse profusely. Then, still grumbling to himself, he ordered the radio to be bought to him. Starr prayed this time that Casey would use a frequency monitored by Helena. Despite his tendency to mumble, Starr could still make out the words he spoke into the mike, and the female response was very clear.

"Yvette, this is Glenn small change in plans. We had a flat due to Ed's incompetent driving and lack of proper planning." Casey glared at Ed while he cowered even more "everything quiet at home?"

"Quiet as a cemetery," came the response.

"Good, we will come in on foot and should be there by dawn. The girl is feistier than I expected. Better send some of the boys to the village to collect her brothers. I want some extra insurance. By the way, there are only two seems her daddy already fried one."

There was a slight pause and then an unemotional "Whatever you say, sweetie, how many men should I send?"

"At least five fully armed and kill anyone who gets in the way, but I want those boys alive. They do me no good dead."

"Consider it done," Yvette replied "I will have a good meal waiting for you. Over and out."

Casey replaced the mike with a grin on his face and turned to face Starr. "Well, my dear, a slight delay in reaching your father's workshop won't hurt, and as you heard, my insurance policy should be quite effective. I may even let you all live after this. Nick could use a new younger woman, and the boys would make good houseboys. So now you will walk and fast each time you try to escape will be an extra beating your brothers will get. I also will take off your gag, and I really don't want to hear a word from you, or I may release Nick on your brothers. The things he can do with his knife would look like mighty pretty artwork on their baby boy faces." Casey's laugh was sinister, and Starr felt a chill to her spine, knowing he meant every word of it. Nick's grin at the prospect was enough to convince anyone that cooperation was the best route and Starr nodded a submissive assent.

Casey did not even give her a chance to allow circulation to return to her hands, and he was off leading the way with Nick in charge of her co-operation. It was a long exhausting night with only one rest stop, and at dawn, they crossed the last hill before the Fielding home. Casey's camp was on that hill, providing a perfect view of the house below. Yvette was frying up eggs on the fire and showed some compassion when she handed Starr a plate. Casey growled, but Yvette's reply was. "You've practically worn her out. She needs strength to keep a clear mind. After all, Martin may have booby-trapped the place."

"Just don't go getting soft on me. I like you the way you are." Casey's response came as he crammed eggs in his mouth.

As Starr ate, savoring each morsel, she observed only three men besides the three that had traveled with Casey. Her odds were improving, and Casey had no idea of her real strength or the surprise waiting for him. The flat tire had put the timeline back in place, and she scanned the mountain looking for signs of Calvin but not expecting to see him. Jason had taught him well.

Calvin was perched in a tree watching through binoculars. With the sun on his back, he knew not even a reflection would give him away. Scott had called just after the group had entered the tunnel, so Calvin had passed his job onto Diana and raced back to grab Ginger and a spare horse. He worked his way to his present perch tethering the horses in a nearby cave. He was grateful this area was riddled with caves and tall leafy trees. The Maple tree he was in actually had a semi-comfortable crook to sit in. Just before he arrived, Scott called to tell him of the updated plans, so after an ugly-looking group of five on horses passed by him, Calvin took the opportunity for some sleep, knowing the sun would wake him.

It did, and he was now alert, observing the camp closely. Starr looked OK, and he did not see Charles. He prayed that it did not mean he was dead. Calvin still did not like him, but he was helping. Calvin still wished he had a picture of the look on Eric's face when they told him he had been drugged via his wake-up coffee and not told of the escape plan, so his reaction would be natural. However, he had convinced the villagers and the stranger, and that was all that was needed. He knew that by now, the equipment that had been pilfered was on its way north, and the twins were safely underground. The unknown was Casey's reaction and Starr's ability to escape.

As Calvin continued his vigil, Jason observed from just south of the camp. He was mounted on Gregory, ready to Gallup in if necessary to provide a distraction. That flat tire had been a God send, and he felt confident the plan would work too bad that it would not now cause Casey's demise as he had hoped, but of course, they could not jeopardize Starr.

Casey stood suddenly as he swallowed the last bit of eggs. His men were not done but knew better than to disobey his silent order. The dogs moved in to finish the rest as they put their plates down. Nick grabbed Starr, and they headed down the Hill to the Fields home without talking. Starr had been so cooperative on the trip that his guard was relaxed. After all, how far could this slip of a girl get with six men guarding her?

Calvin hit the button at just the right moment, and the subsequent explosion took Casey's group entirely by surprise. All dropped to the ground except for Starr, who bolted southeast. She was halfway across the field before Casey's men pulled themselves together to give chase. Yvette had observed the whole scene and was mounting up to pursue. As she scanned the field to get her bearings, she was surprised to see a rider break from the trees and head for the fleeing girl. In amazement, she saw the rider lift the girl on his horse and gallop off away from the now burning house and Casey's camp. The girl's lead was now too great, and Yvette turned her attention to Casey and his men. Calvin, observing the escape, rode off to the pre-arranged meeting point to meet Jason and Starr. It had been a successful mission.

CHAPTER 30

A WEEK LATER, while Casey and his men were licking wounds to their pride and trying to sort through the remains of the house for anything useful, all others returned to the Protectorate. Charles moved into Jason's original room and started taking daily sessions with Dr. Carr to see if he was an appropriate candidate to be a Brother of the Order. Rachel and her brothers moved permanently into the castle and started formal class work. Su Lynn, Ben, Helena, and Ron packed all belongings and moved permanently north to prepare for the western group's arrival.

It was a public departure with a commissioning service by Dr. Carr as they went north for more contemplative prayers. The Monday after, Scott had a meeting in his office with Richanda and Jason, and to his surprise, he requested Calvin be present.

Scott was amazed at Calvin's rapid maturing to adulthood. As he waited for the trio to arrive, he contemplated that spring day when he had Richanda send Calvin to collect Jason's things. The carefree boy had been replaced with a young man who, although not yet sixteen, showed high maturity levels. He hated to include him in the next step of their venture, and yet he dared not to. He had to face it despite his youth, or maybe because of it, Calvin was key to the next mission, but could he expect him to take the risk?

Scott's musings were interrupted as the trio entered his office precisely on time for the meeting. Their precise arrival was Richanda's doing; he smiled inwardly as he greeted them.

"Well, have the three of you come off the clouds yet, or do I need to pop your balloon with reality."

Calvin was still quietly respectful in his presence, and Jason still could not tell when Scott was joking or serious, but Richanda knew him well and grabbed his hands and spun him around while shouting joyful exclamations regarding their success.

As Scott caught his breath, he motioned them all to sit down. "Now, with all the packing and traveling, we have not had time for a full report, so let me have your impressions of the mission, Calvin, you first."

Calvin cleared his throat and replied, "Rachel is certainly calmer and less concerned over safety. But, of course, it helps that Casey recalled his men. Unless Casey wants revenge, they should be safe. I watched his reaction as the house blew up, and it was shock and dismay. He did not even attempt to chase Rachel or Starr, I should say. I think Ray and Charles need to stay at least the winter here or even safer up north. Although I still do not trust Charles completely, I trust his loyalty to Rachel, not necessarily to us."

"Good observations as always, Calvin, and what was your perspective, Richanda?"

"The equipment is safe up north, especially once the four "contemplatives" arrive, and it will certainly give us plenty to work with as we try to reverse the damage. I am not sure, though, that we should not just destroy it and let nature take its course in the re-discovery of science. No one was stranded in Space like when the Soviet Union broke apart, so what was our hurry? But, on the other hand, that equipment in the wrong hands could be dangerous. How well can we trust the motives of the western group? After all, the man who invented it could not change the damage what makes us think we can. In other words, I feel worried about having it."

Scott sighed. "I, too, feel that weight of worry. We may destroy some of the equipment, but the memory switching device is useful for interviewing future visitors. The drugs were so dangerous, and the lasting effect was unknown. Your worry about the west is also founded. Jason, we trust them because we trust you, but a lot may have happened in five years. Any insights or helpful words to ease our tensions?"

Jason paused as he evaluated his response. "To be truthful, Scott, I don't know. I have actually been thinking of that as this time has approached. I think our trip from the pickup point to their new home will tell us much, but Helena and Ben should not reveal the underground initially and only to those who prove trustworthy. I think my group needs to learn how to live like a villager before they try to balance the high-tech stuff."

"Good advice Jason." Scott replied, "And similar to what I was thinking. Actually, that is why I wanted Calvin present at this meeting." Calvin's ears picked up, and he became really attentive as Scott stared at him. "Calvin, again, I find myself faced with asking you to make some pretty adult decisions. I would appreciate you joining the trip to find Jason's group. I need you to lose your high-tech maturity and become a carefree thirteen-year-old that adults will ignore and talk about things they would not share with us. But, before you respond," as Scott cut off Calvin's enthusiastic response, "there will be danger. We hope to only at most travel one hundred to two hundred miles, but we do not know precisely where they will land, what other mercenary groups are out there, or if Casey's group will give us trouble. This may be the most dangerous thing you have ever done."

Calvin paused a moment and then responded, "Sir, I'm in as much danger here from Casey's group, and if I can help prove Jason's group is OK, it's worth it. I will be honored to be part of the team if my dad will allow it."

Scott nodded approval as he replied. "I took the liberty of asking your father, and he said yes. That is settled, then. But, Jason, I can only spare Calvin and Richanda with school in session. Will that be enough?" Jason nodded the affirmative "Good. One horse each as a pack animal and your standard mounts. Once you find the group and radio in a specific location, we can send horses and wagons. I'd like you to leave at first light the day after tomorrow so Calvin Starr is expecting you so she can give you lessons on acting thirteen and stupid. Richanda, you're in charge of supplies, and Jason, let us confer more over these maps. I want to set up some prearranged meeting places and locate the most logical landing spots." Scott stood to indicate Richanda and Calvin's dismissal, and as usual, his abrupt dismissals took one's breath away.

As they walked down the hall to the elevator, both were silent, contemplating the meeting. Richanda broke the silence. "A cup of sugar for your thoughts, Calvin."

Calvin laughed and readily responded, "I'm not sure they are worth more than a loaf of bread, but I'm also not sure I would share them with anyone but you or Jason. I'm scared, Richanda."

Richanda stopped her quick walk to the elevator and diverted Calvin to a small lounge area they had passed. As she sat down and looked at Calvin, concern was written over her face and her mind flooded with worry. Her first words almost sounded harsh as she released her concern. "Calvin, if you were scared to go on this mission, you should have said something. You do not have to prove anything to anyone."

Calvin took a deep breath to put his thoughts in order and almost whispered. "It's not the mission that scares me. It's that I'm growing up too fast. I love spying around with you and Jason, but I'm more comfortable with our community's adults now than with my peer group. Yesterday Frank wanted to play some ball, after only ten minutes I was bored, and we did not even have anything in common to talk about. A year ago, he was my best friend. I should be in class with all the kids my age, but I am going for acting lessons instead. I like it, I enjoy it but will I someday regret not playing ball with Frank or thinking of ways to torment Sharon?" Trying hard to hold back a sob, Calvin pleaded with Richanda for an answer with eyes that were still youthful but mature as well.

Richanda gently placed her arm around his shoulder, laying his head on her shoulder in a motherly fashion as she sought for words of wisdom for her young friend. She wished he had been scared to go on the mission.

"Calvin, we all grow up or mature at different rates and for different reasons. You were destined to grow up fast when your mother died. Your father tells me you took over the laundry and meal making while he worked long hours at the hospital since you were only five. That is a lot of adult stuff. You have always had the edge over your peers for that reason. Just because Frank Fitzgerald is eight months older than you does not mean he's as mature as you. Years ago, when I was on the fast track to early graduation, I worried I would miss my senior year activities in high school. While my friends were getting ready for the prom, I was doing final exams for my first year in college. Although glad, I was pursuing my goal. I thought I would regret not having that memory to share with my friends. Do you know what? I went to my five-year reunion expecting to not be on the inside crowd cause I missed it all, but everyone was too busy talking about what they had done after school, and I fit right in. The moral of my story is pursue what you know is right for you. Don't compare to others, but if you want to go back to being Calvin Q kid who hates Mr. Wells English lit class, I can have Scott take you off the mission, no questions asked."

Calvin broke away from her hug and looked her in the eye as if to judge if she was serious or not. Although the silence seemed to last forever in Richanda's mind, it was only a few seconds before Calvin's reply.

"No, I would be too busy worrying about the two of you getting into trouble without me along, and besides, I hear a big term paper is coming up I wouldn't mind missing."

Richanda tussled his hair, and he grinned a fifteen-year-old grin as the two returned to the hallway to prepare for the adventure ahead.

BOOK III

CHAPTER 31

To the average mind-warped villager, they appeared to be a typical gypsy family traveling from village to village, trading books and telling tales. Although no one had seen them before, their tale of hard times up north due to drought satisfied even the most cautious, and the man told good tales around the table at the Inn while the wife taught the women folk home remedies. The boy, well, no one paid much attention to him as he did chores for his parents or the merchant who put them up for the night. Their cover story was perfect, allowing them an excuse to travel and to ask questions about the road ahead, "seeking out the right village to trade wares in," and the only legitimate reason to enter a city to forge for new books. Even the occasional mercenary group ignored them as they had no interest in books.

They had been on the road for three weeks and had been in fifteen villages and three former cities. They were so far from home that no one in this village had even heard of the Slippery Creek protectorate, which was the largest one south of New Hope. Jason and Richanda were engaged in their usual diversions to try to glean information while Calvin performed chores for the innkeeper. Most from the protectorate would never recognize the trio. To prevent later recognition, they all had dyed hair raven black, and Calvin had contacts to change his blue eyes to brown to match his "parents." Jason had shaved his beard, and Richanda kept her hair so tightly braided it gave the illusion of being perfectly straight. With it pulled back tight against her face and with the right makeup, it did not look like his friend at all.

He was helping Jed tonight, the Innkeeper's son who was twelve years old and the first real bright child Calvin had met outside of his home group. They had just finished feeding and watering the animals and were taking a break before cleaning the barn. After three weeks of hard labor and no nibbles, Calvin was beginning to regret not staying for the term paper, but he laughed to himself, thinking that he could now shed his reputation of being a wimp when it came to working. Jed motioned him out to a knoll in the yard to have a drink and a bit of cheese. As they stared into the night sky, Jed broke the silence.

"Kevin, did you ever wonder about the lights in the sky? I mean, are they lamps or worlds like ours."

Calvin was instantly alert for both clues or a trap and responded cautiously. "I always thought they were lanterns in the sky lighted by the Gods, but then a crazy woman came to a village we were in and called them planets. She said she could fly like a bird up to them, but the crowd stoned her for heresy. So my Ma says not to concern myself with such things. What do you think?"

"I think they are planets, and I think that man can fly to them. I read a lot and not only books that are legal but the ones about science. I do not remember much about life before this Inn, but I remember living in a house that lit up without lanterns, and I rode in a box that went up and down. I lived in one of the tall buildings above the clouds in the forbidden cities. Father forbids me to talk of these things."

Calvin interrupted, "Yea, you might be the next target practice for stone throwing. It's not a pretty sight."

Jed became serious. "No, I know my mother was stoned. You see, she was a scientist and still believed in science. They found out. I was seven, and I remember Dad grabbing me and running with me as the mob took mom away. They had come for all of us, but mom was on the porch and warned Dad. We traveled for two months before we settled here. Dad still cries at night sometimes, and so do I."

Jed and Calvin just stared into the night sky, not knowing what to say, but somehow comfort was exchanged in the silence. Both boys had to blink to confirm what they now saw. Some of the nightlights were moving. Jed was the first to break the silence. "Kevin, it's a plane."

"A what," said Calvin, although in his mind, he was already using his math skills to plot its course to report to Jason.

"It's an airplane. It flies like a bird, and I bet it's landing in the forbidden city. So quick, let's go tell dad and the village."

"Are you crazy" Calvin shouted "Even if you are right and these strange lights are this plane, you talk of what will that get you but a beating. Tell no one, or the Gods may be angry."

"Kevin," Jed looked at Calvin pitifully, "I thought you might be a high tech, but I see you really are a mind-warped gypsy. I can't let you tell my secret to anyone." Suddenly Calvin's innocent friend became a knife-welding enemy. Calvin danced and avoided each thrust while pleading for his life.

"Honest Jed, I'll not tell even my Ma."

"Sorry, Kevin, dad and I have it good here. Can't afford to slip."

"But Jed Ma and Pa will look for me, and you'll be found out."

"No, Dad will deal with them and say they moved on. We need to protect ourselves."

Calvin had danced Jed back to the barn, where he remembered a shovel was propped. Jed lunged at him, and Calvin rolled to the side, grabbing the shovel in one fluid motion. As Jed prepared for the next lunge, Calvin swung the shovel hitting Jed square on the forehead. Calvin grabbed the knife and ran, not even stopping to see if he was still alive. As he rounded the corner of the Inn, Jason and Richanda were bidding the owner a good night saying they preferred to camp out tonight. Richanda saw Calvin and quickly responded to his signal.

"Calvin, are you alright you look like you've seen a ghost and been in a fight."

"I almost was a ghost," gasped Calvin.

Jason had joined them and directed the pair to walk down the road away from the Inn.

"I think I just killed Jed. He's at least a high tech, possibly a mercenary, and after he told me he was high tech, and I acted mind warped, he tried to kill me."

"Calvin, are you sure he's dead?" asked a worried Richanda.

"I don't know. I hit him with a shovel and ran"

"Why didn't you tell him you were a high tech" Queried Jason.

"I thought it might be a trap. He was too good with a knife and thought nothing of killing me."

"OK, Calvin, what's done is done. I will sneak back for our horses and supplies, check on the boy, and then we disappear. Meet me at the fork in the road but keep covered." Jason immediately disappeared, and Richanda and Calvin continued down the main street until well out of human sight. Once off the road, they doubled back to the secondary road, which headed east, and hid at the fork a mile out of the village.

As they hid behind a rock waiting for Jason, Calvin relayed the whole story, this time telling of the plane. "Do you think I killed him? I had never killed anyone before. What else could I have done?" Calvin was beginning to break under the strain, and Richanda felt useless.

"Calvin, listen to me. You did what seemed right at the time. You can always think of a million solutions after the fact, but you cannot go back and change the facts, so you need to accept right now that you did your best. We'll ride to the city when Jason returns and look for this plane."

Calvin took her words in and mulled them over as they waited for what appeared to be an eternity. Jason finally arrived with all the horses in a parade behind each other.

"The boy still lives," He proclaimed as they mounted, "and will be unconscious for a while. I reported finding him when I went to check on the horses. I said it looked like an accident that the shovel fell on him. They will not know we have gone till morning; by then, we will be long gone."

"We have a destination, Jason," Richanda replied. "Calvin saw a plane head for the city over the next rise."

They were off riding silently and quickly. The road was dry and rock hard, so Jason had little worry of leaving a trail. But, again, a perfect plan was going wrong, and Jason began to worry.

CHAPTER 32

THE MOON HAD been just about full so they could ride well into the night. A few hours before dawn, they could see the city and stopped to set up camp. They had no desire to enter an unknown city in the dark. Calvin had been especially silent, and Richanda worried about him but decided to let him be for now. As the trio settled for sleep, they found it difficult because of the excitement of possibly ending the mission or because of the disturbing events of the previous evening. For whatever reason, they awoke with the sun, not feeling in the least bit rested. Breakfast comprised of bread, water, and an apple for each, as they did not want to risk a fire. Jason was more concerned about other groups the plane may have attracted and was fearful of using the radio for fear it would put his friends in more jeopardy if mercenaries were present.

As in most of the cities, they searched the airport that had once been outside the city, but the city encroached upon it, and in the case of this city engulfing it, so it seemed to almost be located in the center. The three knew the routine well as they entered the city and headed for an area that might hold a library or bookstore. They soon found a jackpot 3-story store. Unfortunately, it was so damaged that all that remained of its name was an AL and a NS at the end. Calvin usually enjoyed trying to guess the name of a store, but this time got right to work pulling out the right kind of books to fit their cover story. He even found a book on horses that he decided to save for the Fields boys. Once loaded up, they headed down the street, not appearing to be going anywhere, and lazily made their way toward the airport. They spoke casually in normal tones discussing the fine haul of books and what they could trade for them to sustain them through the winter. To an unseen observer, they would appear to be wandering merchants without a care in the world, but under the brim of his hat, Jason's eyes were darting to all corners seeking avenues of possible ambush and escape.

Richanda's hand on the packhorse's load was not to steady the load but to pull the tranquilizer gun out if needed. Although she abhorred violence, Richanda was a crack shot. In fact, it still irked Jason that she was better than he. They were walking over a former expressway overpass, and from that vantage point, Jason spied the plane sitting in the middle of the runway, or what was left of the runway. Seven years of neglect had taken its toll, and Jason's opinion of Dudley's flight skill went up several notches as the plane appeared still intact. They were still too far to see clearly, but it looked like the plane's occupants were camped under the plane's wing, cooking a meal. Despite a desire to rush over, the trio kept their leisurely pace, even taking a detour around a collapsed section of the road rather than appear intent on their destination.

As they passed through the remains of a fence, Richanda pointed to the plane and said. "Oh, look, Jared, another group camping out. Maybe we can join them and trade."

Still cautious of onlookers, Jason hailed the group they were approaching, now recognizable as friends. "Hallow there, well, met strangers. May we share your fire and strange shelter?"

A man who Richanda later found out was just thirty but looked in his mid-forties stepped forward. "Well, met, please join us for a meal and a story to tell us where you have been.

We are a large caravan and welcome news of other villages to assist us on our travels."

Jason's group had learned discretion well in their years of hiding and were taking Jason's lead. Although now under the wing, Jason realized they were still within earshot of a hanger. Mercenaries still used high-tech listening devices, so he introduced using the aliases they had devised.

"I am a traveling peddler of books. My name is Jared, and this is my wife Rebecca and son Kevin."

"I'm the leader of this band of families, Jared, Webster Nolan's the name, and this is my wife, Florence."

Jason shook Web's hand, and then his wife, Richanda, and Calvin followed suit. Upon closer examination, Richanda realized that Webster's features looked younger than his mostly white hair indicated. She could see the strain on each man's face as they refrained from having the kind of reunion they desired. Finally, everyone came round for introductions: Dudley and Susan White with their five children, James Rogers, the doctor, and Bob Lawrence, the dentist. The Paulson's Richanda picked up before introductions. The doctor and nurse couple were exactly as Jason had described, and with his dark hair and olive skin and her brilliant red hair and fair complexion, they were hard to miss. Joan Cole looked like a lot of fun, and Andrew Davis was the image of his sister Julie and had the sparkle in his eyes of his sister Starr. She longed to tell him his sisters lived but dared not, just as they had not told Julie or Starr until they could be sure. However, she had no doubts now. She was not as sure that Douglas Morrison was related to Sandra-Jean, but she tried to look for family features as she shook his hand and that of his wife, Grace. They were not meeting the children yet, but Grace was very pleased to introduce her two-year-old Jason, and Richanda did not miss Jason's surprise and delight as he met his namesake. Steven Baldwin was the quiet type, and

Nancy Mimm, the slender blond with hypnotic eyes, more than compensated with a bubbly personality.

Richanda had lost count, but she thought she had met them all when a tall, commanding presence appeared in front of her, apparently from nowhere. He had the most expressive eyes and stared directly into hers as he gallantly took her hand and kissed it.

"Webster, please introduce me to this striking beauty, and I pray she is not married to the man who accompanies her."

Web Laughed. "Tom, you rascal, if you had not been wandering off, you would know that this is Rebecca, wife of Jared and mother of Kevin. Tom Malone is our resident Casanova and recently joined our group."

As he shook Jason's hand, he apologized for trying to steal another's wife. Richanda was still catching her breath as she was trying to decide if she wanted him to know the truth or not.

Webster offered lunch that was being prepared, and as they sat to eat and show off their bounty of books, the serious communication began. As Jason was showing off each book and extolling its praises, Web was reading the written instructions on the inserted paper they had prepared while in the bookstore. The plan was to publicly part ways after lunch, and Jason's group would head south and Web's group north. They were to meet again at a shopping mall just inside the city line, enough to keep the locals away but close enough to the woods for a quick escape if needed.

Just as Richanda thought that this entire charade was a waste of time, a jeep rapidly approached the plane with two men who appeared on the surface to be unarmed. As if on cue, the children ran and hid behind crates and moms' skirts, the incriminating papers became fuel for the fire, and the men broke out the bows and arrows that Richanda had not even noticed. Richanda clung to her family bible.

Web stood forward and hailed the jeep as it came in earshot. "That's far enough, stranger. State your business. We mean no harm, but we will defend ourselves."

The jeep pulled to a stop, and the passenger stood up. "Now, that's not the way you greeted these other strangers, or are they not strangers to you?"

"They did not approach in a mechanized vehicle as you do, may the television curse you, so these strangers were well met. But, again, what do you want?" Web stood forward as he spoke, and Dudley and Andrew took up positions on either side of the jeep with bows drawn. Jason could see no others, but danger could come from any of the buildings that were scattered on the tarmac of this small commuter airport. Neither occupant was recognizable to Richanda or Jason, which was a relief, but the next moments of silence seemed like an eternity spent balancing on the head of a pin over hot coals.

"I am the governor of this fair city, and this is my second in command." the leader said with a sarcastic laugh, and his driver snickered. "We were staying at the country mansion when we saw your plane land last night, so we drove up to collect our airport taxes," As he finished, he wore a menacing smile.

"I fear you are out of luck as the occupants of this plane, as you call it, are gone. We are travelers from a distance merely passing through and also came to seek information from the people in this strange vehicle, but we arrived this morning to find them gone and shelter from the sun, our only reward for going out of our way. I understand your job as governor and collecting taxes, but as we did not land in your airport, and we are armed, and you are not, I feel a fair levy can be agreed upon."

The leader responded, "And do you think I would approach a group of high techs unarmed? I am no fool." And with a wave of his hand, two more jeeps appeared with two occupants, each armed with machine guns from the rear. They had slowly approached while all eyes were on the governor. Web stood his ground and continued negotiations.

"We can still kill you with the arrows as my men are experts as this is our food source. We are not, as you call us, high techs, but we outnumber you. All we desire is to continue our journey without losing all our possessions. This vehicle had crates we could not carry, and we will share them as payment. You may be able to overpower us and get it all, but I assure you that at least two of your men will not come out alive. Is a thirty percent loss of personal worth one hundred percent of goods that may even be worthless to you?"

Again, the silence was filled with tension as each group sized up the other. The governor abruptly broke it with a belly-wrenching laugh. "Put your guns away, men. We have been outsmarted by a smart group of mind warps." Each one placed his gun in the back of his vehicle and placed hands on the windshield to prove they were empty but kept the sneer on their faces. Finally, the leader stepped out and approached the group to assess his taxes. The bows stayed armed and pointing.

"Now I put my weapons down. That's not very neighborly of you to keep yours up."

"Well, now, Mr. Governor, I've been around enough to know that yours can be up and shooting before we restring, so we'll just keep loaded, but my men have good strong arms, so don't worry."

The "gov" kept the same smile on his face but approached slowly, keeping an eye on the two yeomen closest to him. With all eyes glued on the two leaders, no one noticed the children. Calvin and the Paulson's son James were no longer with the group. During the initial scurrying, Calvin pulled James behind a barrier created by the wheel of the plane and some boxes on the opposite side of the plane from the rest of the group. When the other two jeeps arrived, they positioned themselves at 4:00

and 8:00 to the group, and with slow, careful moving Calvin and James were now behind each jeep. James was not the eldest child of the group. In fact, he had just turned ten, but Calvin had seen the mischief in his eyes when they met and felt the risk was worth taking.

Now with the leaders playing word games, Calvin had James positioned behind the jeep closest to the plane, and he had the other one. No other adult had seen their movement's intent as they were on diplomacy. Still, ten-year-old Pam Rodgers, holding the Morison's youngest baby, Hope, had and was watching the occupants of the jeeps for any sign of noticing the junior saboteurs. Calvin retrieved his guns without a hitch, but as James reached over for the second one, it slipped and made a slight noise. Only because Pam pinched Hope so hard that the baby screamed, no one noticed James. The boys quickly retreated to their hideout, and Pam quieted the baby.

The governor had finished his inspection and was pretty upset. "This is just farm tools and clothing. There is nothing here I can use. I need guns and ammo and computer parts. I have no use of bows and arrows, and I do not farm. You mind warps are pitiful. You don't even steal the right books. (Referring to Richanda's pile at her feet) He turned abruptly and jumped into his jeep. As he backed away, he yelled to his men. "Waste them." Arrows flew not at human targets but at the wheels of the jeeps. Other group members pulled out blow guns and aimed them at their would-be attackers. Not finding their guns where they had left them, they quickly succumbed to the tranq darts. The governor took to running and was out of distance of the blowguns but not Richanda's high-powered pistol, which had been in the cut-out pages of her Bible.

Within a few minutes, the captives became the captors, and six sleeping bodies were in front of them. No further activity was seen in the distance, so either this was the entire group or their friends were assessing the situation. Although pleased with the outcome, all the adults were puzzled that the guns had not been used when Calvin and James came out with sheepish grins and submachine guns in each hand. Richanda was the first to break the stunned silence.

"Calvin, that was entirely too much of a risk, but I'm grateful for the outcome."

Having laid down his arsenal, Calvin put his arm around James's shoulder and said with a twinkle in his eye. "You know, no one ever pays attention to us kids. By the way, perfect timing on the baby cry" Pam nodded in acceptance of the compliment and blushed.

The Paulsons were hugging James as though he had actually been injured, and Jason threw Calvin the look that said, "I'm proud." Then, Webster got right to business.

"Our tranq's last four hours. How long are yours?"

Snapped back to the here and now, Richanda responded. "About the same, but also wipe out recent memory. I will dose up his companions; they will never know what hit them when they wake. Jason load them up in their jeeps and drive them to the other side of the airport in a hanger. Take the horses so you can ride back quickly. We want to prevent memory recognition if they wake up near the plane. Web, you can load up your group. We can only take essentials, but the horses can carry some as we will leave the books behind. Calvin, take your new friend and bury those guns in the field over there. We'll leave in one hour."

Jason laughed inside as Richanda's take-charge attitude sounded so much like Scott, and her effect on the crowd was the same as his. Dudley and Tom offered to accompany Jason, and the rest got to work.

Despite everyone working quickly and efficiently, it was still a large group to organize seventeen adults, eighteen children, and Calvin. Richanda could not figure out what category to place him in, so he became the Calvin category for now. It was well past noon when the group finally started, and the days were getting shorter, so they did not dally. The westerners had bought two large carts that Jason attached to the pack animals' saddles, so they could bring more of the group's possessions than expected, and each adult and child over five had a backpack with private property. They looked a bit like a military campaign, but Richanda figured they would avoid all villages between here and home to avoid too many questions.

Just before they left, Web and his wife pulled Jason aside and gave him a backpack to wear. He looked inside and broke down momentarily. When he returned to Richanda's side, she questioned what was in the pack. "Jason, what is in your new backpack, something from home?"

"Yes, they bought my few personal possessions that I did not dare carry on the trip, including a portrait of my wife on our wedding day and a personal photo album. We did not have much, but this is precious."

"Oh, Jason, I am so happy for you. I know how much you loved your wife."

"Yes, but the ghosts are fading into fond memories. We need to go now."

Jason and Richanda were pleased with the organization and speed that the group moved despite so many small children. Richanda again pondered the life these children had led, always hiding on the move, always in danger. Only the youngest had been affected by the incident; the rest treated it as business as usual. The children at New Hope were fortunate indeed to live in relative safety and be able to grow up children. Richanda thought back to her research paper for child psychology. She remembered the black, dark pictures they drew when they first entered the refugee camps, but she also remembered the pretty rainbows and flowers and children playing in later years. Hopefully, soon these children will feel safe enough to play and draw rainbows. She was bought out of her musings, as Jason wanted to plan as they walked.

Jason, Richanda, and Web were in the lead, with Jim Rodgers and Dudley White in the back. Calvin was in the middle with all the children. Although several years older than the oldest, he blended right in as Starr taught him. They were almost out of the city, and the plan was to travel till there was no more light. Jason began the meeting.

"Web, you've gotten the group into good shape. How far can we push them?"

"Well, Jason, life was difficult after you left. I'm sure you noticed that Jacob didn't make it stoned by villagers when he was discovered in a city stealing parts for the plane." Jason took on a stoic expression and nodded for Web to continue. "We have learned a lot about keeping alive, and everyone, including the children, have been on forced marches and heavy-duty field training the last three months. They can manage whatever they have to."

"Good, if we can do twenty-five miles a day, we should reach New Hope in twelve to thirteen days, and North Creek is another four days beyond by horse. So, we will have you all in your new home in less than three weeks. By the way, we built you a new home called North Creek, so get accustomed to that name. The group is too large to integrate without question, so we will set you up north and rotate you through New Hope as needed."

"Jason, this is more than I could have hoped for." Responded an awe-struck Web, "You are handing us paradise."

"Not quite Web, the group will need to take on the persona of a religious group and follow some strict rules of conduct to fool the locals. There are no locals yet, but in a few years, there will be. Being Brother Jason took some getting used to, but it is worth it. Do you think Tom Malone can act like a pious man of the cloth?"

"Don't worry about Tom. He is just overcompensating for the death of his wife. We found him holed up in a cave six months after mercenaries raped and killed his wife. He has been with us for two years, and I trust him. And as for the rest of the group, it will just be so good to settle in one place that abiding by the rules will be a walk in the park. And most of us are believers anyway, so really not a problem."

Jason then turned to Richanda. "Do we have any health concerns to be alert for as we travel?"

"Safe water is my biggest concern. This is a large group to keep hydrated. The cooler weather will help, but everyone must get enough fluids. I don't think we will be gone long enough to have a parasite problem, but we'll treat everyone when we reach base."

Jason nodded, and they fell into silence, and the march continued till just past dark. They camped near a stream, and as soon as they were settled and cooking dinner, the trio from New Hope disappeared. When they returned, Web almost called the men to arms, but Jason's hail prevented that. Starr had given them a chemical to strip the dye out of their hair; Jason cut two inches off Richanda's hair, and once washed, the curls bounced back despite the three weeks of abuse. Calvin's freckles shone through without makeup, and his blonde hair was the most significant contrast from the black. They had even changed their clothing to their habits and burned the very distinctive gypsy clothing they had worn. Jason felt they could even walk back into previously visited villages without a second glance, but they did not plan to test that theory.

He had radioed Scott, who would meet with the group just south of New Hope with horses and wagons and take them to their new home, allowing Jason and the crew to return home.

As Jason settled down to sleep, he breathed a sigh of relief. Something was finally going well, and even though he felt at home with the group at New Hope, it was good to see old friends again. Imagine Doug and Grace naming their son for me; he thought as he drifted off to sleep. Everyone slept well.

CHAPTER 33

As the group marched north, a routine developed. Twelve-year-old Dalton White and eleven-year-old Douglas Morrison Jr. were in charge of the children, and Calvin, in keeping with his assumed role, obeyed their every command. Calvin's apparent lower status did not affect James's opinion of him. On the contrary, he followed his every move and absorbed his every word. Observing the relationship, Richanda felt it akin to Jason and Calvin's and also knew Calvin would be a good role model.

Each day the women cooked while the men went hunting and foraged for food, and the older children picked dry twigs for the fire. Richanda and Jason slipped into farms on the outskirts of villages they had visited to trade their remaining books for eggs and milk. After a long day of rapid walking, each night around the fire was a long-anticipated rest for the feet and the mind. Jason and Richanda filled the group in on life at New Hope, and their new friends told stories of life out west and the last five years. Calvin sat each night and drew portraits of the adults and children of the group. His skill was natural but had recently been refined by Michael Alden, who had studied portrait art prior to studying architectural design.

Just as Calvin had learned to disappear in a crowd, he could also do his artwork without his subject being aware, except for James, his ever-faithful companion. However, Calvin did overhear the occasional interesting adult conversion, such as the women talking about the group almost splitting up and going separate ways two years ago or the men discussing who would be in charge and how closely did, they need to follow these new rules with Bob Lawrence especially not wanting to wear the habit. Calvin was pleased to see that Web Nolan had as good control and command of his group as Scott did and could reason with the dissenters, but he felt Bob would always grumble about the habit. However, the children were the most revealing of the group, and mid-way through the trip, Calvin reported his impressions to Jason and Richanda as they walked ahead of the group to "scout out" the area ahead. Of course, once out of earshot, Jason started grilling Calvin.

"Well, my young friend, I've missed you these last few days, but what have you found out?"

Calvin jumped into his report with enthusiasm and organized clarity of thought. "I agree with Web as leader of the group, and I would trust him with the underground immediately. According to Dalton, Nancy Mimm is almost a villager and resents the fact that we are trying to save technology. He says her attitude started when her husband Jacob was killed getting airplane parts. According to the women, the only reason she stays with the group is to get help caring for her daughter Samantha born after Jacob's death."

"Doug and Grace Morrison are solidly behind Webs leadership, but Dudley believes he should be the leader as he has more education, but according to Doug Jr. and Thomas, he is too unsure of himself and wavers on decisions. Even Dalton says his dad can't make up his mind. Bob Lawrence is a bit of a rebel and may find it challenging to keep up the ruse. On the other hand, Andrew Davis is the perfect junior Dr. Carr. All the kids call him a Bible thumper and say his whole backpack is filled with only theology books. Not even extra clothing beyond one change."

"Joan Cole is very picky about her cooking and will only let Pam and Jane Rogers help her because the other kids "cannot do it right." She also has her feelings hurt easily, so don't complain about her cooking if you want to eat the rest of the trip. Dr. Jim is wonderful and as easygoing as his daughters. He seems to be a real caring doctor, but he also has some good leadership skills, so I vote for him as head brother next to Web. On the other hand, Steven Baldwin is a real computer geek and may be their version of a cloistered brother cause puters is all he talks about, and Tom Morrison says he sneaks computer games on City trips. Web frisked him before this trip, but he may be a danger in the future." Calvin stopped his monologue for a breather, and Jason and Richanda, who had absorbed it, all walked silently for a moment. Jason broke the silence.

"What about the Paulsons with James as your shadow? You must know something?"

"To be honest with you, Jason, that makes it harder. No one says anything bad about them in front of James, and he adores them. From the adults, I pick up that they are both good in their profession and well-liked, although Gerald is a perfectionist. They had problems having children, and James is their only one, so his mom does dote on him a bit."

Then Richanda jumped in. "And what about Tom Malone?"

"Yes," Jason added with a raise in his eyebrow. "What about Tom Malone?"

Calvin paused, looking at each one, and, despite his youth, realized a triangle was forming and smiled before he answered. "He reminds me a lot of you, Jason."

Jason balked. "That scoundrel. I seriously doubt your judgment on that, Calvin; we are not alike at all."

"Au contraire, like you, Jason, he suffered a deep hurt, and all his flirting is to keep from hurting just like you keep busy to keep from hurting."

Jason fell silent, and finally, Richanda changed the mood. "Great assessments, Calvin; you truly are a good spy, but how do you think the children will adapt to their new life?"

"I think the seven that are four and under will have no problem and will more than likely forget the plane ride. I would trust the Morrison kids and Nolan kids as well as James with the underground eventually but let them all settle in first. In fact, besides Andrew Davis, they will all need help adapting to their new life, so keep it low tech first."

Jason laughed. "I'd better watch myself, or soon you will knock on my door to take over my head Brother's job." And they all laughed.

The trip proceeded without a hitch, although heavy rains near the end slowed things down. They were a day late meeting Scott who had bought Sandra-Jean and Julie. The Davis and Morrison reunions were happy events, and Andrew was excited to find out that Starr was waiting for him at North Creek. Scott had sent her North for "safety" after the deception, and the villagers thought it was a good idea, and she loved helping the construction crew put on the final touches. Andrew had not seen his sister since before she went to boarding school for fine arts majors and was not sure he would recognize her but was anxious to try.

Jason, Richanda, and Calvin felt at home with the North Creek group as they were now calling them. Still, Jason was relieved to return to New Hope without Tom as he was paying entirely too much attention to Richanda, and she was enjoying it too much. As they parted company to head home, Jason felt carefree, like he had not since before his wife's suicide. The acute pain of her death was gone, but the loneliness remained. It had been almost ten years since her death, but with all that had happened in his life, it seemed an eternity ago. Since her death, he had always had a purpose or goal; either to find her killer, find New Hope and finally bring the two groups together. The question was could he become a farmer living in a religious community? Would he enjoy the peace after so many years of high-stress activity living on the edge, or would he quickly become bored? Then, of course, there was still Casey to deal with but hopefully not for a while.

They were close enough to home that Calvin had ridden on ahead to see his father, so Jason and Richanda rode on in quiet musings. Richanda broke the silence. "Cup of sugar for your thoughts."

"Oh, nothing worth that much. Just wondering what I'll do to keep myself busy from now on. You have Rachel to train and your medical work; Calvin will go back to school. So what does a former secret service agent do in the New Hope community." And Jason sighed, waiting for Richanda's response.

"Oh, don't worry. Scott will find a job for you, and there is a lot to do to incorporate North Creek into a functioning community, and the danger from Casey is not over. If anything, once his pride heals, he will be back to torment us in force. And of course, you could spend some time looking for a wife. I know a line would form if you indicated interest."

"You mean to settle down and start a family of little ones running all over?" Jason responded in mock surprise.

"Yes, I mean just that. You need a namesake with McGregor on the end, not Morrison. Your too good with children not to have your own."

"Your right, Richanda. I may be ready to settle down, but only if you are on the top of the list."

Richanda blushed and kicked her mount onto a full gallop as she yelled, "Only if you beat me to the stable."

Jason joined in the race, and they arrived at the barn entrance in a dead heat. Nevertheless, there was much laughter and horseplay as they groomed their mounts and returned to the castle to prepare for the evening meal.

CHAPTER 34

THE MEAL THAT night was a festive one. Two nights previous, Dr. Carr, had announced David and Nichole's wedding and Harvey and Cindy's. It was to be a double wedding and the first the order had had, so Scott was sent North to invite their sister group to the house raising and festivities. The village was buzzing with all the happy news and a general air of excitement. The village could not wait to meet the northern group and were so excited to have such a happy event occurring. The harvest had been good, the men injured in the logging accident had recovered with only mild physical limitations considering the severity of their injuries, and the double wedding seemed to be the perfect final celebration before life became isolated for the winter.

Everyone was glad to see the trio return from their journey to evaluate young Calvin to see if he was worthy of taking vows. The villagers were quite pleased to hear that he would be vested as a full brother at the wedding. Richanda was glad to see Calvin eating dinner with Rachel and was pleased to see her maturing before her eyes. Without the physical danger taking its toll on her, she was becoming more independent and assertive. The report from Tim was that she was a first rate-nursing assistant, and he felt she could start an apprenticeship with all the nurses to be a fully qualified nurse.

As Richanda ate the best meal in weeks, she watched as Sandra-Jean, who had returned just before dinner, huddled with the engaged couples planning the wedding reception with Jenny to ensure their plans were reasonable given available resources. Sandra-Jeans husband, Frank, on the other hand, was going over plans for the newlywed cottage and the joining staircase for Cindy and Harvey with the innkeeper who was coordinating the acquisition of the needed raw materials.

The lumberyard was giving all needed wood as a gift to the couple and to the protectorate that did take such loving care of them, requiring nothing in return. Joel, the innkeeper, was also the unofficial mayor of the village and considered himself the official liaison between the village and its protectorate. His generous gift was two kegs of premium wine and lodging for all the guests. He had already posted the invitation on the tavern board as the entire village was invited.

Dr. Carr lectured the older children on the requirements for joining the Order as Calvin's decision spiked some interest, and Frances was flitting from table to table trying to figure out music selections. As Richanda's gaze fell to Jason across from her, she was surprised at the frown on his face contrasting with the general air of gaiety. "Jason!" She snapped in surprise. "We are planning a wedding, not a funeral. What is wrong?"

"Oh, I know I should be able to relax, but I have this inner suspicion that danger lies ahead." He continued as Richanda tried to interject. "No, there is no concrete reason for my feelings, just a suspicion that our open invitation may be an open invitation for Casey or some of his cohorts to join us. I do not want our guard to be down. Remember, Robin Hood used a wedding to rescue Fennel so she could marry Allan-a-Dale."

Richanda sobered quickly. "You're unfortunately right. It was a harvest picnic open to all that precipitate Adam Lane's death."

"I know this thing between New Hope and Casey goes way back, but how did it start?" Queried Jason.

They had finished eating, and Richanda motioned they should take a walk. It started to rain again, so they went to the library. Mark was the only one present, so as they picked a secluded corner to talk in, Richanda gave Mark a mute signal, indicating their conversation was not to be overheard by villagers. Even though no one could hear them, Richanda spoke in almost a whisper.

"Rachel's story actually helps to put a missing piece into the puzzle. We could never figure out how Casey suspected we were high techs, but his connection with the network explains things. You see, Adam Lane was a crack investigative reporter for the newspaper. He was outstanding, winning many awards. He used to joke that if he had been born female, he should have been named Lois Lane. In fact, that was almost Jenny's name, but Jessica won out."

"Adam was the spearhead of our group's investigative branch and was instrumental in bringing down the network. Unfortunately, his picture was next to his byline in the paper, but in all the confusion during that time and the rapid digression of people's minds, we did not think it would matter or that he would be remembered. Adam was our group's original leader and got us organized and prepared for the life we now lead. Sam was his pastor, having retired from traveling, so that is how he was recruited. It is probably because he founded our group and defined our cause that he was willing to die to keep it going. It's still such a waste."

Richanda paused to compose herself, and Jason sat in silence, not wishing to push her. In a few moments, she continued. "It was early spring of 4 AT, and we were almost done with the castle. We were here before any villagers, so as each family moved in, they naturally turned to us as a logical protectorate and never questioned, which is what Jessica predicted. It took us so long to build because we also helped the villagers build, and we needed to use primitive building techniques, at least for exterior work. Although we had accomplished a lot on the underground facility that winter, we were not yet prepared to meet visitors as we met you, and we learned a lot from our encounter with Casey."

"Casey and his knife welding friend Nick rode into town, and after a drink, at the inn and a friendly talk with Joel, they came over to greet us. Nothing seemed out of line in his greeting, and if he recognized Adam, then he didn't let on. It had been four years since Adam's last article, and he had grown a beard so that Casey may have recognized him later. Who knows? We only know he did. Casey announced that we would be neighbors as his clan was moving in over the next ridge. We welcomed him warmly. Casey and his men were in the village often that spring and summer. They came for a beer and relaxation but always stirred up some trouble. We were tolerating it until early September when Nick raped May Butters. She was only fifteen."

Jason thought about the young girl he had seen walking in the village with a child constantly in her arms and her eyes always downcast. The villagers had rallied around her and supported her, but she felt the shame of the event and the robbing of her childhood. The only males she trusted were her father and Dr. Carr, who had done extensive counseling with her. Jason mentally put Nick on his list of those he meant to deal with. Richanda continued through his musings.

"Casey was banned from the village and his gang. Nick had escaped barely from an outraged mob, so we thought we were finished with them for good. But unfortunately, we were lulled into a false sense of security. In retrospect, Casey was obviously building up his men, his arms, and his plans. The end of October, we had a harvest cookout inviting the whole village to have one big celebration before we hibernate for the winter. Similar to what this wedding will be, so I see your point for concern.

Adam Lane was a committed believer, so not only was he committed to the cause he knew where he was going when he died. When Glen strapped him to the electric chair and told him he would flip the switch if he did not like the answers, he kept our cover to the end. As he saw Glenn go to throw the switch, he mouthed I love you to his wife. I am sure his only regret was that his wife and daughter had to watch his execution which is what it was. Pandamonium broke out as the villagers and the mercenaries broke out in conflict, and George Myers was shot in the confusion. So the next day, we had a double funeral."

Jason sighed and looked Richanda in the eyes as she softly cried. "I know you abhor violence and murder, but Glenn Casey and his cohort Nick do not deserve to live."

"I know that, Jason, but the violence must not come from us. Remember, vengeance is mine saith the Lord. So we need to be defensive, not offensive."

"Your right. Of course, I just hope to defend myself against the man someday." And Jason's face turned hard and cold as he spoke.

Suddenly a large book dropped on the floor, and as Mark loudly apologized for the noise, a group of village girls came into the library to do some studying. Jason and Richanda continued their conversation about wedding plans. But, unfortunately, both now had a lot on their mind, none of which pertained to the happy side of wedding plans.

CHAPTER 35

TIME SEEMED TO fly even for the engaged couples, and the day of the house raising dawned crisp and clear. With the leaves at the peak of their color change, the whole village exploded in color. Everyone prayed that the wedding day would be as beautiful. The foundation had been dug, and the basement poured over the two weeks since the announcement of the wedding, and the north Creek group had arrived the afternoon before looking refreshed and already blending well with New Hope. At the break of the day, the men started working on the construction of the frame while the children looked for the best nails that had been raided from the nearest city. Their nimble fingers allowed them to sort the straight from the bent nails as they made three piles: straight with a point, straight needing sharpening, and bent needing straightening. The older children put on the points and straightened, and it kept them out of trouble while feeling useful. Although most of the women were involved in preparing the lunch for the workers and for the reception, Starr and a few others were seen pounding in nails and swinging from rafters.

With the villagers and the North Creek folks helping, the tasks were quickly accomplished, and by lunch, the cottage was totally framed and the roof half done. The mood was happy at lunch as everyone mingled and appeared to be celebrating the wedding a day early. Nichole just kept wandering through the half-done building discussing last-minute changes with Frank and David. They only needed to enclose the home and complete the kitchen and bedroom as the rest could be done over the winter. So, there would always be room for changes, David kept telling her.

Just before everyone returned to work, Carson Tibbs stood and cleared his throat for an announcement. Carson was the local blacksmith and kept kind of to himself, but Harvey had befriended him. He even had Cindy teach his children to shoot, good enough to hunt. But, like Harvey, he was unaccustomed to public speaking, so he stuttered and stammered as he started.

"Uh, oh well, as you all know, Harvey and I are pretty close, and well, ever since Stephanie died, Cindy has kind of helped with the young'uns even though they were not too young so well I didn't want them to have just a plain wooden staircase so well anyway come on out boys and show em."

From around the corner of the building came Carson's sons carrying an intricate circular iron staircase. A grapevine was hammered in relief out of the iron between the rail and each step. Cindy cried at the thoughtfulness of the gift while Harvey just speechlessly hugged his friend. The whole community applauded the fine craftsmanship. Carson turned red but was pleased with the response.

Jack and Helen Brady stood next, and Jack spoke for his whole family. "Well, as long as it's time to be giving out gifts, my family and the Hales, Blacks, and Moore's have a gift for the couples. I know we gave the lumber for the building, but we are so grateful to everyone at New Hope for taking such good care of us that was hurt and our families while we were laid up. Well Ed is really good with a chisel and Philip is good at making furniture, so we made you each a bed. Zack and I milled the lumber so we would have a part too." The rest of the Brady, Moore, Black, and Hale families bought around the two beds, and more tears and applause followed. Jack continued over the applause. "Oh, and even though we had to delay things a bit to let Philip get all his strength and thinking straight, we want you all to come to Philip and Mary's wedding next spring." Which, of course, bought more applause and shouting.

"And" Helen Brady banged a spoon on the table for attention. "Not to let the men folk show us up, the village women have started quilts for the couples, but they are not done. But, by spring, we promise they will be done." And the ladies of the village spread out the two tops that were all pieced except for the borders and, of course, still needed the tedious job of quilting. They were both the wedding ring pattern, but someone had gone to much trouble to determine each couple's favorite colors, and each quilt was perfect for the couple for which it was made.

Nichole and Cindy were speechless as they went around hugging each person responsible. Finally, David rose and commanded attention. "I'm speaking on behalf of my precious bride-to-be and for Harvey and Cindy when I say we are overwhelmed by your generosity. As members of this religious community, we are committed to helping people everywhere. Still, we are also glad to be a part of this greater community and pray we can always serve you. Thank you for loving us as we love you. God Bless."

As David sat down, Joel stood up. "Well, if everyone could hold back the rest of the gifts till the wedding, we have a house to build and a staircase to install. Light is wasting, so stop procrastinating and get to work" Everyone laughed as they cleared plates and returned to their jobs. By sunset, the cottage had been completed with all but one room, the future nursery, so there was no hurry, and the staircase was installed. Furniture was moved in, and David and Harvey prepared to spend the night at Dr. Carr's.

As everyone settled in for a good night's rest, Calvin and Rachel went for a walk around the lake. The weather had turned cool, so each had a wool cloak over their habit. In the dark, from a distance, no one would have been able to tell who they were or that their habits were student gray. (Rachel wore gray when not on duty in medical) They were beyond the chapel but could still see the building when they came to Calvin's favorite place. It was an exceptionally large flat rock set on land that jutted into the lake. Sitting on it, you felt like you were on an island surrounded by the water, which gently lapped against it on its way to the stream that led away from the lake. Calvin helped Rachel up, and the two laid back and just stared into the starry heavens for a long time. Calvin broke the silence.

"You know, I'm kind of glad this whole thing happened to society because we could never see the stars because of all the lights in our city. Let's not make cities in our new world."

"Yea, mom, and dad liked the stars too. Dad always said on the top of our hill, looking at the stars, he was closest to God."

"I'm sorry, Rachel. I didn't mean to remind you of your folks."

"It's OK, Calvin. It's good to remember now that the horror is gone." Replied Rachel as she squeezed his hand in reassurance. They sat in silence for a few more moments soaking in the stars and the silence. This time it was Rachel who broke the silence. "Calvin, when you take vows tomorrow, will they be real or fake? I'm not sure I understand that part of our cover."

Calvin sat up to make eye contact in the partial light of the moon reflecting off the lake, and so did Rachel. "For me, they will be genuine. Dr. Carr and I had a long talk just after he returned from his crusade, and we blew up your home. I had a long talk with him because I wanted to ensure it was real. He helped me sort out some of the issues I was having about the facts and emotions I was telling you about. He explained the path to becoming a Christian and the need to be one, not just ride on your parent's faith which I guess is what I was doing. He explained the whole salvation thing to me as if I knew nothing which was best. Once he laid it all out, it became clear to me that I needed to surrender to God and give my life to Jesus, and I have become a Christian. I am glad I made the commitment, but I still need to learn a lot and do more growing in faith. Of course, all these adventures are sure a faith grower to be sure. Richanda and I spent much time on the trip to find the Northern group discussing spiritual issues, so I feel better grounded."

"Dr. Carr really is a Christian preacher and only agreed to become our figurehead leader if he could genuinely evangelize the villagers. That is why we have the church, Sunday School, prayer meetings, and Summer Bible School. Every adult who is a part of New Hope on the outside had to be considered a member of the Order to maintain our cover. So far, new people have been considered a part of the north branch when they were absorbed into the group, so this will be the first formal vow-taking ceremony. Now that there is really a north branch, the villagers have met, I guess we will have more in the future. Dr. Carr knows who is serious about their vows and who is not; for instance, Ben Rose is Jewish, so Dr. Carr will not marry Ben and Helena. He's pretty old school about mixed marriages. Su Lynn is Buddhist. They each have rooms below with all kinds of stuff from their respective religions. In private, Dr. Carr has lengthy discussions with them, but the deal with Adam Lane was no pressure. Only those committed to their vows are allowed to teach Sunday School and stuff. That is why Su Lynn usually has a medical call on Sundays, and Ben only teaches Old Testament history to the New Hope adults."

Rachel interrupted. "So, what caused you to speak to Dr. Carr?"

"Humm, I guess in a way, I've always believed in God. I remember mom reading me Bible stories before she died, and

I remember being mad at God for taking her away. We stopped going to church then. Dad was strung out too, and then all this device stuff started. Dad told me he recommitted soon after things started up but wanted me to find faith on my own. Ever since Jason arrived, my life has been stretched, and I've needed to trust in something. Like when I found you, that was a scary time, and I prayed, but I was unsure why or if it would work. I wanted to have the same faith as Richanda and my dad. Now you want to talk with someone with strong faith, talk with Richanda. Why all the questions?"

"Oh, I'm not sure I guess I'm searching. Dr. Carr said I do not have to take vows to stay as a nurse. Especially since my brothers and I were rescued from the wild, and the villagers accepted us without being a formal part of things. Mom always read from the Bible, and our names were straight from the Bible, but dad always said he had no time for formal religion, but God was in his heart, so I am bewildered. I cannot even consider taking vows till next summer cause Dr. Carr said I need to be under his teaching for a year before I decide. Charles became a Christian while you were away and is truly a changed man. He spent a lot of time with Dr. Carr and asked many questions regarding faith and the need for a changed life. Once it was explained to him that he was a sinner and needed forgiveness, he gave his life to God. He intends to take vows next summer, but I do not think he will ever learn the underground. In a way, he will be the only true "Brother of the Church." But he was so bad before that he needed it. I have always been good; I had no chance to be bad, so I guess I'm confused. I don't want to take vows just to take them. I want to believe in them, but I don't know what will cause me to."

"Dr. Scott once told me we all mature at different rates physically and spiritually. I have had all the background knowledge most of my life, and you have not. So give yourself a chance to catch up on the info and keep searching. Dr. Scott said in the end, we each make our own decision, and no one can force us. You might talk with Richanda; you two seem pretty close."

"Yes, I guess we are, and yes, I will. Thanks, Calvin. I appreciate your insight."

They spent a few more moments in silence and got up to walk back slowly to the castle. They had just rounded the bend in the road and could see the castle when Rachel was suddenly grabbed from behind with a knife at her throat. It was a lone attacker, but the knife's position prevented Calvin from doing more than initially react. Rachel froze in silence. The voice from the blackness spoke in almost a whisper.

"Tell your fellow cult members that if they know what's good for them, they'll call off the weddings and prepare to meet Casey. He's coming to take over your little operation."

Calvin had recovered his wits and lowered his voice as he replied. "And why are you warning us if your one of his group?"

"Even mercenaries have a heart, and I've got kin in the village, and I don't want them hurt. Our war is with you, not the village. Now stand still, or your woman dies."

He backed up slowly, and just as Calvin was about to think he was taking a hostage, he threw Rachel down and ran into the night. Calvin called an alarm and ran for Rachel.

CHAPTER 36

It was midnight before everyone had calmed down enough for a meeting in Dr. Carrs's office. Almost the whole New Hope community had been roused, and most were crammed into Dr. Carr's office, making him wish he had opted for the conference room.

Jason was plotting defenses while Richanda was fuming over the disruption of the happy event. Nichole was crying in the corner while David tried to console her. Webster Nolan and James Rogers were present, the rest of the group were staying at the Inn, but they had been with Dr. Carr and were the first on the scene when Calvin sounded the alarm. Scott and Jason were questioning Calvin and Rachel for the umpteenth time, and both were holding up well, proving how much they had matured in the last months.

"Now, Calvin, are you sure you could not identify your assailant?" Scott asked, pacing like one of his fish.

"It was dark, Dr. Scott. I thought it might be Nick because of the knife, but he was too short, and the voice wasn't right. But, of course, mine sounded different too. He was more nervous than Nick would have been, and I don't think he knew who we were specifically."

"What makes you say that?" Queried Jason.

"He told me to tell my fellow cult members, not my parents, and he called Rachel my woman. With our cloaks on, you really could not tell a student's habit from a regular one, and it was dark. Rachel never said a word, and I lowered my voice, so he likely has no idea who he talked with."

"That's good." Mused Scott as he talked while he planned. "The story will be that Alex and Jonathan went for a walk and were the ones accosted. Alex is close to Rachel's build and color, and the hair is a perfect match, which would have been the most seen by our mystery man. Jonathan is a bit taller than Calvin, but hopefully, he will not know the difference in the dark. For all we know, someone in our loving village family may knowingly or unknowingly be a Casey spy. Nichole, David, Cynthia, Harvey, with your permission, we will still have the wedding."

With that, there was a noticeable gasp in the room. "Yes, that's what I said. This is plain terrorism, and we cannot bow down to it. But, unfortunately, all who can will bear arms for this wedding. Sandra-Jean, you will tell the tale at the well. Let them know the wedding is still going on, but we will be careful with security. It is now a closed wedding only those we know well can come to the chapel. Web, Casey does not know your group, so I want you all in regular clothing and sit with the villagers interspersed. Any other suggestions will be gratefully accepted."

David beat Jason in his response. "I suggest a dawn hunting party to scan the area. The wedding is not till 11:00, so we can scour the area and be back in time."

"Excellent idea. Jason, you are in charge. Pick a team and do a complete search in the morning. Then, Web, you can go back to the Inn and fill your group in. I want all children to be watched closely and do not let them wander. They will be safer at the wedding; a child as a hostage is a nasty thing."

Jessica raised a timid hand, which Scott acknowledged. "I know Dr. Carr trusts him, but do we trust Charles during all this?"

"That's a good question, Jessica, but I think we not only have to trust Charles, but we need to arm him. Casey will not be pleased with him and may eliminate him first. Ray can hide out in the library, and Charles can too if he wants, but Ray was more specifically threatened, so he has no option, and as a Mennonite, he refuses to bear arms. So, Rachel, you and your brothers go underground."

"Excuse me, Dr. Scott." Rachel cut Scott off mid-thought, which he was not accustomed to, so he looked quite startled at Rachel. "I agree that my brothers need to be underground, but Starr is in more danger than I, and I want to fight for my safety. After all, I, too, have a score to settle with Casey, and I would hate to miss my chance." Her voice never wavered, and her eyes were set with a look of determination that Scott had no choice but to agree. He nodded in the affirmative as he continued laying out his plan.

"Tim, Richanda, I want the back chapel loaded with medical supplies just in case, and Mark and Diana load with extra weapons. Make it a public stocking, so if Casey is watching, he will know we are prepared and hopefully turn tail and run. Jenny, the reception is now indoors, even if the day is beautiful. There is more control that way, and we will block access to the upper levels. That covers the basics any questions, see me privately. Now everyone go to bed. I want you all fresh tomorrow. Volunteers for the morning search meet with Jason before you leave. Dismissed."

As Calvin left with Jason, he was amazed at how much comfort he now gleaned from Dr. Scott's abrupt dismissals. It was as if that was one thing that was constant and could be counted on. His father had leaned over and told him in no uncertain terms was he to volunteer for the morning search, so he took on his old job of Rachel's protector and planned to be her shadow as much as possible.

This was not a sudden unexpected danger or behind-the-scenes subterfuge, and despite the cockiness of youth Calvin was surprised to find he was scared. Jason had announced the meeting would be in his room at dawn so the North Creek group could be present. They were the only two left waiting in the lobby. Jason seemed relaxed, almost cold, as he was mentally prepared for the next day. Calvin did not know what he was thinking or feeling, but he knew he had to have his feelings expressed.

"Jason, what is it like to get hurt? I mean bad hurt by a weapon and maybe almost die."

Bought back to the here and now by the question, Jason stared at Calvin as he had started up the stairs but then thought better of it. He led Calvin to a bench in the garden on the now deserted ground level of the castle. "Calvin, we are forcing you to grow up too soon. It hurts and is scary, and you never get used to it. Do not let all the adults fool you; we are all scared, but we do not plan to hide all our lives. We are not indestructible, so keep your head down if shooting starts. If it helps, we are defending versus attacking; this is our turf, so we have the advantage. Remember, George Myers was shot in the confusion that broke out. It could even have been a village bullet for all we know. Casey's advantage is he knows when, where, and how. So you concentrate on defending Rachel and staying alive, do not be distracted by anything else. It wouldn't hurt to send a prayer upward, either. Richanda tells me you are on the side of faith, and that is good. We need people who know how to pray since I don't. And don't go telling Richanda she will figure it out on her own soon; she is close enough, and no, I do not want to be converted now, my friend. Especially if I get a chance to defend against Glenn and Nick."

Calvin responded with a pensive OK as they crossed the lobby and climbed the stairs in silence, Calvin deep in thought and Jason wondering if he had said the right thing. Tomorrow would be an interesting day, and he prayed to some higher authority that a funeral would not follow the wedding.

CHAPTER 37

IT HAD RAINED hard that night, which would have given the hunting party an advantage, but the hard rain had also bought down many of the autumn leaves covering all trails and possible tracks. After three hours of searching the village's perimeter, they found nothing. Sandra-Jean had discovered that Hazel Cotton's son was more than likely the one who delivered the message. Her son Derek had left two years ago to seek adventure out west. No one else knew, but he had sent word to Hazel three months later, saying he had joined Casey's group. Hazel was a devout woman who, as a widow, was raising five children. She was ashamed of her son's lifestyle and actions. After revealing her secret to Sandra-Jean, she went straight to Dr. Carr to ask forgiveness.

It was a relief to know that a spy was not among the village, and no one was shocked that Derek had come to no good. However, pity was the overwhelming emotion felt towards Hazel. Everyone knew how hard it was to raise children alone in this world, and the damage from the device did not help. They knew Hazel had tried to raise him by the Good Book, but some slipped through.

The chapel never looked so lovely. Grape vines had been twisted into hearts, with wildflowers grown in the greenhouse twisted in. The effect was a heart-shaped wreath of flowers, and with several gracing the pulpit and first few pews, the chapel took on a multicolored appearance. Fabric banners were strung from wall to wall creating a colorful ceiling, and everyone wore their best for the celebration. The members of New Hope were all in full habit and sat in the front pews. Although no one had told the villagers that North Creek would not be in habit, no one questioned, nor did they question, the extra security and weapons check at the door.

As Calvin peeked out the spy hole in the door of the robbing room, he could feel the tension in the church. People were talking in hushed whispers and laughing nervously as if to dispel the gloom with fake gaiety but not successfully. There was such a difference from just twenty-four hours ago. Starr had given herself and Rachel a complete makeover, and neither looked like themselves or the Rachel that Casey would recognize. Calvin was surprised to see Hazel Cotton in the congregation, so as he turned away from his vantage point to help Dr. Carr with his robe, he queried the minister, who was also deep in his own thoughts.

"Why did Hazel Cotton come? I'd have thought she would stay at home and safe."

"Oh, Hazel, yes, Hazel, well, she feels she may provide some protection for the children as her son will not harm her at least and may keep any conflict away from her. I tried to tell her it was not her fault, and his path was already set years ago, but she feels so guilty. I also tried to tell her it was a blessing because it gave us a warning, but not even that helped. She is punishing herself more than anyone else could. Calvin! Don't tie that so tight!"

"Oh, sorry, Dr. Carr."

"That's better now. I can breathe when I say the marriage vows. Maybe I should put off your vow taking till you can tie a good knot."

Calvin stared at Dr. Carr with a look of surprised fear for a split second before he saw the laughter in Dr. Carr's eyes, and they both laughed, and for the moment, at least the tension was gone.

The pastor whispered, although no one else could hear them in this room. "I'm so glad your vows are real, my friend. You will make a fine Brother of the Order."

The chimes sounded the 11:00 hour, and Calvin and Dr. Carr walked out to the podium. Calvin stood in front of Dr. Carr and Jason and Richanda joined him on either side as Dr. Carr addressed the congregation.

"It is not assumed that all the children born to the members of our community will meet the requirements or have the desire to take holy vows. Nor is our Order limited to those born from our group. Anyone who professes a faith in Christ, meets the educational requirements, and can demonstrate a true calling to the life we lead is welcome. Today we are gathered for three joyous occasions, the first being the vesting of Calvin Timothy Barnes as a full Brother of the Order of The New Hope. Calvin has met all the requirements and proven that he is worthy of the responsibilities that will now befall him. Although it will be another month before he turns the legal age of sixteen, his father has consented. Therefore, although Calvin and I have spoken at length, it is now appropriate for him to make public vows and for you, the congregation, to uphold him in those vows."

"Calvin Timothy Barnes, do you now vow and proclaim that you are a Christian and vow to live your life according to Christian values as laid down in God's holy word?"

"I do."

"And do you, Calvin Timothy Barnes, agree to live your life dedicated to helping your fellow man and especially reach out to the poor and widow?"

"I do."

"Then, as God's servant on this earth and leader of this community, I welcome you in as a Brother of the church and ask all assembled here to recognize his status and support him in his new role."

There was a generous round of applause, and Calvin blushed despite his desire to remain serious.

Dr. Carr continued. "All new members of our Order are assigned two persons to help learn their duties. Although Calvin will finish his last year of school, his responsibilities will increase, and Brother Jason and Sister Richanda have agreed to be Calvin's sponsors. They will now assist him with his new robe. Calvin will be apprenticing in animal husbandry, explaining the tan color, but he also is an accomplished artist showing talents in portraits, therefore the lavender border. When he graduates, he may someday teach your sons and daughters."

As Dr. Carr addressed the group, Jason slipped Calvin's tunic over his head, and Richanda clipped the belt on. Jason shook his hand, and to Calvin's embarrassment, Richanda gave him a big hug and kiss as she cried. Again, the group assembled applauded as Calvin took a seat in the front row next to his father, who was beaming.

Calvin had wanted to savor every moment and retain every sense to remember someday. The smell of the flowers, the crispness of his new tunic, and the sound of whispered congratulations as he sat down, but it was all over too soon, and now everyone was turning to the back of the chapel as Cynthia proceeded down the aisle. Paul Welsh was giving her away. They had actually met at the last Olympics as Paul was on the equestrian team, but he was not as fortunate to bring home the gold. In fact, he had been Cynthia's first suitor after things had been established, but the sixteen years between them were too much of an obstacle for Cynthia to overcome. Nevertheless, they remained best of friends, and he was honored to be the one giving her away to the man she loved.

Although everyone was looking at the bride, Calvin glanced over to see Harvey. He looked uncomfortable or at least out of place in the tuxedo-like suit the women had made him, but he had eyes for only Cynthia and had the biggest grin on his face. It was as if she was the only person in the room. Ron Schmidt was standing for Harvey and Richanda for Cynthia. The vows were exchanged, and after a long round of applause, the newlyweds sat on the first pew for the second wedding.

Cynthia had been happy but not nervous. Nichole, on the other hand, was a basket case. Despite her veil, Calvin could tell she was crying as she walked down the aisle on Dr. Scott's arm. David also looked nervous, and although he looked happy, Calvin did not think his smile was even close in size to Harvey's, which was still off the scale. Jenny, of course, stood for Nichole, and Eric stood for David. The ceremonies were identical, and Calvin felt his mind wander until Dr. Carr proclaimed the couple husband and wife. Calvin had expected everyone to be dismissed at that point, but Dr. Carr had David and Nichole sit while he addressed the congregation.

"Friends, we have had three happy events here today. We pray this joyful day does not turn ugly, but we know the possibility exists. We must remember today that Casey has started this conflict and keeps it going. We have never shone any aggression towards him, nor will we ever. So remember, friends, it does us no good to be on the attack. We will only defend ourselves and ask our friends in the village to do the same. And now may I introduce Brother Harvey and Sister Cynthia Stotts and Brother David and Sister Nichole Douglas."

There was no receiving line, and everyone headed straight for the castle. Gerald Paulson and Bob Lawrence had stood watch and greeted the guests directing them to the dining area.

The party and the feasting lasted all day. The food and wine flowed, and the village musicians joined the New Hope musicians, and everyone danced in the foyer area. As the hours went by, all forgot about the threat.

It was just dusk, and candles were being lit in the overhead chandeliers. Everyone was sitting in small groups visiting or dancing to walk off the feast. Tom Malone had just whisked Jenny off to a lively square dance that had started. The moves were crisp and fast, and soon a crowd had gathered to watch the dancers and cheer them on with clapping to keep time with the musicians. As Tom and Jenny were doing some fancy footwork that required their attention to perform correctly, an arm reached out of the corner where the candlelight did not quite reach and grabbed Jenny by the waist. Thinking it was Tom making a wrong move, she turned to scold him and looked into Nick's face and the point of a knife. Jenny fainted as the room was flooded with light from all the lanterns in the hands of Casey's men, who suddenly filled the room. Nick had dropped to the floor to continue to hold the knife at Jenny's throat. The silence was immediate as everyone had their eyes glued to Jenny and Casey as he walked in with a big smirk on his face. Then, feeling very much in control, he addressed the gathering with a loud booming voice.

"How pitiful this rag-tag group of religious sissies is. They can't even defend their women who faint at a moment's notice. So now Nick won't hurt her unless you decide not to cooperate. Now, who leads this group?"

Dr. Carr stepped forward from the dining room with a look of controlled furry, but Casey waved his arm flamboyantly before he could speak. "Not you preacher man, the one who tells everyone where to go and what to do."

Dr. Scott spoke quietly from the library doorway as he walked toward Casey. "I guess you mean the administrator of the Brotherhood, and I would qualify as that. Although Dr. Carr is our leader, I will speak for us both. What do you want? We have done you no harm."

"What do I want? What do I want?" Casey tapped his fingers together as he spoke. "I want to be rid of you high techs in disguise, and then the village will be mine."

Before Scott could answer, Joel, stepped forward into the space in front of Casey. "You have no proof these people are high techs, as you say. You could not prove it when you killed Adam Lane, and you cannot prove it now. These people are our friends and our protectorate from disease and ignorance. They are a valuable contribution to the life of this community. You are a leech, so leave us all alone."

Casey appeared to ignore the speech as he continued. "Fancy words, bar keep, but if I prove they are high techs, all you superstitious fools will turn on them, and I will have my proof. So, Dr. Scott, if you value this lady's life, come here." Scott boldly stepped up to face Casey. "Now I found a lie detector in town. It works well. Put it on, and we will see what happens."

In confusion, Scott looked at the wires, and Casey, in disgust, motioned for one of his underlings to attach the machine to him. "Now, to demonstrate, Dr. Scott, what is your full name?"

"Scott Elias Jenkins."

"And your profession?"

"A Brother of the church and senior administrator of Brotherhood business."

"That has all been the truth." Casey snarled. "Although I suspect the last was only a half-truth, now tell me a lie, like how many children do you have?"

"I have none."

Casey made a big deal of showing everyone the results indicating a lie. "Now, Dr. Scott, do you have an underground plant beneath this edifice?"

"Yes, I do." was Scott's calm, even answer.

Casey was shocked for the second time in his life, the first being the Field house blowing up. "Why are you telling me this? You should be trying to lie to save your secret."

"Well, Glenn, we would have preferred to keep it a secret from the villagers, but your capture of Jenny forces me to show our secrets. So come with me, and I will show you." As he spoke, Scott walked towards the garden and disconnected himself from the machine. Casey and his immediate guard followed, as did key villagers and members of New Hope. When they reached the center of the garden, Scott moved two pots on top of a large rock, revealing hand holds, and pulled on the rock, which fell forward, revealing a staircase—calling for a light, he offered to take Casey down. Then, looking back to ensure Nick still had Jenny, he stepped down, requiring Joel to come to inspect as a representative from the village.

Shouts of rage and anger could be heard from below, as well as the laughter of Scott and Joel. The momentary confusion was all that was needed. Starr whistled, and tranq darts flew at Casey's men. Jenny, who had never really fainted, but by then was being ignored by Nick as he tired of stooping to guard her lifeless body, hit Nick in the buttocks with a tranq dart she had surreptitiously removed from her habit. Tom wrenched the knife from his hand the moment he was hit.

"I think this will make a lovely addition to your kitchen cutlery, don't you, Sister Jenny?"

Jenny laughed as she stood up, letting Nick fall to the ground unaided. "Call me a wimp, will you? That will teach you."

Casey came storming up, ready to injure the first person he saw, only to look at the pointy end of a pitchfork aimed at his oversized belly. James did not look like he should be messed with. Seeing his men lying in the center of the foyer, Casey quickly became a very meek man.

Having heard the whistle, Joel and Scott came up laughing and drinking. As they neared the top, Joel made an announcement. "Now I know why the protectorate kept this underground a secret. They have been hiding the best wines down there. So now I know where to come for a good vintage."

Everyone laughed except Glenn Casey, who was pitiful without Nick and his men to back him up. Joel continued. "Dr. Carr as leader of this protectorate, what judgment do you pronounce on this man for the crimes he has committed?"

Dr. Carr stepped forward, and the room became silent. He stood in the silence, staring at Casey, who had begun to squirm under his cool stare. Dr. Carr was indeed a man of God whose face always had a twinkle or a jovial smile; however, it was now cool and cold with the look of extreme anger being held back under control. "Glenn Steven Casey, the crimes you have committed against this village and humanity are many. You and or your men have personally hurt the Lane Family, Ruby Myers, May Butters, the Fields family, and who knows the others outside our sphere of influence. In Biblical times an eye for an eye would indicate your execution for the lives you have taken. We are not so inclined to follow the Bible so completely, but you threaten us and others in surrounding villages. We can not in all good conscious allow you to continue your reign of terror."

"When Cain killed his brother, God sent him out but also put a mark on his forehead. In the case of Cain, it was to protect him from being killed, but it also identified him as a murderer. So your judgment Glenn Steven Casey is to carry the mark on your forehead of murderer and outcast so all will avoid you. Your men who are also guilty but are also only followers will receive the same tattoo on their right hand but you and Nick on your forehead where it cannot be hidden. May God judge you for your sins."

The room exploded in applause, indicating that both village and protectorate personnel agreed with Dr. Carr's judgment. It was not a permanent solution, but it was one that would allow everyone to sleep at night. The men were dragged into Dr. Carr's study. Two villager's experts in the craft got busy doing the right hand of all the men. Ben Rose, who was also knowledgeable in the craft, did Nick and Casey's, and his only regret was that they had to be drugged asleep to allow him to work instead of feeling the pain. All were relieved that no funeral had occurred that night. While the artwork was being completed, the dancing resumed lasting well into the night even after the newlyweds left for special rooms at the Inn.

CHAPTER 38

CHURCH HAD BEEN packed with many there to hear about the evening's events who had missed them. Dr. Carr preached a sermon on forgiveness and compassion. Casey's men had woken up damp, cold, and sore on a haystack two miles out of town where their horses were tethered. None were pleased with their new tattoo, and half the group rode off independently to seek their fortunes, figuring they could do no worse alone than they had done with a gang. None of those who remained faithful spoke to Casey or Nick on the way back to camp. It would be a long winter to sulk and plenty of time to plan revenge.

A light brunch had been served, and Richanda, Jason, and Calvin were savoring some hot cocoa as the tables cleared. They sat in silence, allowing the hot liquid to warm them from the inside out, each lost in their thoughts until Richanda broke the mood.

"Well, Calvin, do you feel any different now that you are a Brother of the church?"

"Yes and no, I guess. I feel more committed and responsible, but I do not feel any more holy. I just feel like more part of things. Even though I still need to attend class, I feel more like an adult, but that's cause of all I've done, not yesterday's ceremony."

At that point, Rachel came up, interrupting the conversation. "I'm done with my duties now, Calvin. Want to go for a walk?"

"Sure." Calvin grinned as he gulped his now almost cool coco down and handed the empty mug to Richanda to clean. "Thanks for cleaning this; see you later."

The two walked off, and Richanda leaned back and sighed. "He is maturing faster than he thinks, but at least for now, his future has hope. What do you think, Jason?"

"I think Rachel has the right idea. Let's go for a walk in the opposite direction."

Scott observed the laughing couple depart and let out a big sigh.

THE END FOR NOW

CHARACTER LIST

NEW HOPE PROTECTORATE ─────────────

Dr. Samuel Allen Carr: Age 60 Believer Minister and spiritual leader of the group

Ellen Carr: Sam Carr's deceased wife

Jason Allen McGregor: Age 37 Former CIA agent Non-Believer at time of arrival to New Hope. From the west and brings a group from the west. He appears to take on the responsibility of head Brother from Scott.

Richanda Gray Smith: Age 35 Believer Nurse second in command to Scott.

Dr. Scott Jenkins: Age 50 Believer Psychologist and leader of the group after the death of Adam Lane. Husband of Frances with four children.

Frances May (West) Jenkins Age 51 Believer teacher K – 6. Wife of Scott and mother of 4 children. She also leads the choir.

Dr. Timothy Case Barnes: Age 40 Believer General surgeon head of medical Father of Calvin.

◄ IN SEARCH OF NEW HOPE ►

Dr. Su Lynn Yamoto: Age 38 Buddhist MD family practice She is a specialist in OB and high-risk pregnancies.

Jessica Anne Lane: Age 54 Believer, Sociologist, castle historian, widow of Adam Lane.

Adam Lane: Deceased at age 49. Believer Journalist Spearhead leader of the group killed by Glenn Casey. Father of Jennifer.

Jennifer Lynn Lane: Age 32 Believer Soprano soloist in the choir. Cook in charge of the kitchen.

Nichole Peters: Age 37 Believer Computer expert appears to be cloister Sister as performs data entry. Marries David Douglas.

David Lee Douglas: Age 36 Believer General contractor. Handyman in charge of livestock. Marries Nichole Peters.

Alexandria Rey-Wells: Age 28 Non-Believer Nurse works in medical mother of 3, including 5-year-old twins.

Jonathan Paul Wells: Age 33 Non-Believer Teacher 7-12 Father of 3, including 5-year-old twins.

James Scott Farrell: Age 45 Non-Believer Divorced Lawyer/politician works as a farmer, is the liaison to the village, and is the first contact for strangers.

Helena Ruby Meyers: Age 37 Catholic Widow Electronics expert. Works in library and maintains power plant and solar panels.

George Meyers: husband of Helena Ruby killed by Glenn Casey.

Benjamin Rose (enthal): Age 43 Jewish Concert pianist teaches music and works in the garden without heavy digging.

Franklin Lloyd Fitzgerald: Age 40 Believer Architect organist and designer of community. Husband of Sandra-Jean and father of four children.

Sandra-Jean Morrison Fitzgerald: Age 39 Believer Housewife mother liaison to villagers at well each morning. She is married to Frank and the mother of four children.

Michael Weston Alden: Age 31 Believer Landscape architect designs camouflage for buildings. He has two children and is the husband of Julie Ann.

Julie Ann Davis Alden: Age 30 Believer Marine biologist teaches swimming goes on trips to rescue fish from aquariums, and maintains the fish tank in Dr. Scott's office.

Eric Richter: Age 46 Non-Believer Divorced Nuclear physicist by trade farmer at New Hope. The back story is that he came from the northern community. Has three adult children.

Esther (Starr) Davis: Age 27 Believer Theater Arts major teaches drama.

Paul Cameron Welsh: Age 52 Non-Believer College professor of math and Latin. Equestrian in last Olympics before smashing. Teacher and head of horses.

Ronald John (Yohan) Schmidt: Age 41 Believer Engineer Handyman choir director with Frances.

Mark John Wickersham: Age 48 Believer Librarian head of library and security. Husband of Diana and father of 3 children.

Diana Wynn Wickersham: Age 46 Believer Army Sergeant Head of security trains community in defense. Wife of Mark, mother of three children.

Harvey Stotts: Age 40 Believer Mechanic Handyman farmer and dorm parent to boys. He marries Cynthia end of the first book.

Cynthia G. Black: 36 Believer Secretary Olympic archer took home gold in the last Olympics before smashing. She does data entry and defense training and is the dorm mother to girls. Marries Harvey end of the first book.

CHILDREN OF NEW HOPE MEMBERS

Allen Carr: Age 38 Non-Believer farmer lives in village supports maiden sister. He is estranged from his father.

Jane Carr: 35 Believer Lives in village mind warped and lives with brothers. Loves father.

Colby Carr: Age 30 Non-Believer farmer lives in village supports maiden sister. He is estranged from his father.

Beverly Jenkins: Age 25 Believer grape farmer lives in the village.

Donald Jenkins: Age 23 Believer Adopted son of Scott and Frances. Farmer. He marries Lizzy Welsh and farms up north.

Steve Jenkins: Age 19 Believer On construction team lives with parents

Christine Jenkins: 18 Believer student

Calvin Timothy Barnes: Age 15 Non-Believer at first but converts mid-book. Student. He becomes an assistant to Jason and Richanda in adventures. Son of Dr. Timothy Barnes. His birthday is in November.

Christopher Wells: Age 7 Believer (converted in Sunday school), student son of Alexandria and Jonathan.

Aleshia Wells: Age 5 Non-Believer kid, firstborn twin daughter of Alexandria and Jonathan.

Gillian Wells: Age 5 Non-Believer Kid Second born twin daughter of Alexandria and Jonathan.

Susan Farrell: Age 20 Believer, Daughter of James, lives in the village.

Sharon Farrell: Age 18 Believer student Daughter of James lives in the village with sister.

Frank Fitzgerald: Age16 Believer student

Molly Fitzgerald: Age 14 Believer student

Dan Fitzgerald: Age 12 Believer Student

Mackenzie Fitzgerald: Age 9 Believer Student

Andrew Alden: Age 9 Believer student named after his uncle

Rose Anne Alden: Age 4

Hans Richter: Age 26 Believer on the construction team

Fritz Richter: Age 23 Believer on the construction team. Marries Ruth Welsh

Elizabeth (Lizzy) Ann Welsh: Age 25 Believer Marries Don Jenkins T-8 and farms up north. She is also trained as a nursing assistant to help in medical.

Ruth Welsh: Age 23 Believer teacher assistant Marries Fritz Richter.

Abigail Wickersham: Age 11 Believer Student

Joshua Wickersham: Age 9 Believer Student

Jerimiah Wickersham: Age 7 Believer Student

RESCUED FAMILY

Rachel Marie Fields: Age 16 Non-Believer training as a nursing assistant protects brothers and family secrets. She is rescued from mercenaries by Calvin and becomes his good friend. She befriends Charles.

Matthew Fields: Died year T-5, brother of Rachel.

Mark Fields: Age 8 Non-Believer firstborn non-identical twin computer prodigy student

Luke Fields: Age 8 Non-Believer second born non-identical twin artistically inclined student

Martin Fields (Fielding): Believer Aged 42 at death creator of the device but did not mean for it to be used as it was. He sought a cure but was ordered killed by Glenn Casey.

Alice Fields (Fielding): Believer Aged 40 when killed by Nick.

MERCENARIES

Glenn Steve Casey: Age 45 Non-Believer Leader of the mountain group. Killed or ordered the killings of Adam Lane and many others, including Helena's husband George. Seeks to overthrow Protectorate.

Nicholas Dean Worthington (Nick the knife): Age 35 Non-Believer Second in Command to Glenn. Very good with knives and loves to inflict terror. He raped May Butters.

Ed: Undisclosed mercenary driver for Glenn Casey. Has no backbone.

Yvette Sommers: Age 30 Non-Believer She is Glenn's woman. Loyal and loves him. She was his secretary.

Derek Cotton: Age 23 Non-Believer Eldest son of Hazel Cotton and leaves New Hope Village in search of adventure and stumbles onto Glenn Casey's group and joins.

Charles McAlister: Age 40 Non-Believer Member of Glenn's gang but lazy, so spy's on New Hope and tries to uncover secrets. Rachel befriends him.

NEW HOPE VILLAGE

Elsie Woodbe: Age: 50 She is the waitress in the castle and tavern gossip spreader.

Frank Woodbe: Age52 Farmer frequents pub married to Elsie.

Mrs. Cowman: Age 85 Village widow

Hazel Cotton: Age 47 Believer Mother of 5, including Derek Weaver in village

May Butters: Age17 Believer Raped by Nick fall T-4 when she was 15. Has child Faith June of T-5.

Faith Butters: Age 2. Child of May Butters and Nick.

Carson Tibbs: Age 42 Believer Widower Blacksmith, a good friend of Harvey's, father of 2 adult children. One named Fred.

Jack Brady: Age 45 Believer Logger hurt in accident husband of Fannie Brady.

Phillip Brady: Age 25 Believer Logger Seriously hurt in accident brain injury Son of Jack and Fannie engaged to Mary Hale.

Fannie Brady: Age 40 Believer Jacks wife Phillips mom housewife mother

Ed More: Age 45 Believer Logger caused accident not hurt

Zack Black: Age 35 Believer Logger hurt in accident multiple injuries.

Mary Hale: Age 23 Believer young girl engaged to Phillip Brady

Mrs. Hale: Age 45 Believer mother of Mary Widow 2 other children.

Joel Forest: Age 50 Believer Close friend of James. Owner of Tavern

WESTERNERS RESCUED TO FORM NORTH CREEK ———

Webster Nolan: Age 30 Believer commercial trucker farmer leader of the group. Three children.

Florence Nolan: Age 32 Believer Teacher and mother of three children.

Dudley White: Age 38 Believer commercial pilot farmer second in command, father of 5 children.

Susan White: Age 37 Believer Secretary soprano singer teaches music mother of 5 children.

Dr. James (Jim) Rogers: Age 35 Believer Doctor family practice Second in command until moved south to New Hope. He is a widower with two daughters.

Tom Malone: Age 40 Non-Believer widower respiratory therapist dates every female he sees.

Dr. Bob Lawrence DDS: Age 31 Believer Dentist Learns how to do village dentistry quickly.

Dr. Gerald David Paulson: Age 40 Believer MD ortho with Pediatric residency Head of Medical in the northern community.

Lynda May Paulson: Age 41 Believer Nurse, her specialty is in trauma. Is the head nurse in the clinic.

Joan Cole: Age 36 Non-Believer Dietitian in charge of the kitchen.

Steven Paul Baldwin: Age 58 Non-Believer Divorced He was the top executive micro computers electronics expert who moves south to be around electronics.

Andrew Davis: Age 34 Believer Theology student not yet ordained before smashing Pastor of North Creek Church and figurehead leader. Brother of Starr and Julie Ann Davis Alden. He has a righteous zeal, and children call him a Bible thumper.

Nancy Mimm: Age 37 Believer Widow husband is killed caught stealing plane parts out west. Home care nurse with one daughter. She stays south and marries Tim Barnes T-9.

Jacob Mimm: Deceased killed at age 34 caught stealing plane parts out west. He had one daughter born after he died.

Douglas Morrison: Age:40 Believer Grape farmer. Manages wayside home and plants grape farm makes wine. Has six children, including a namesake for Jason. Brother of Sandra-Jean.

Grace Morrison: Age 35 Believer Grape farmer with husband and housewife and mother to six children, including a namesake for Jason. Village liaison once established.

NORTH CREEK CHILDREN ———————————

Catherine Nolan: Age 6 Searcher student

Maggie Nolan: Age 4 has memories of plane ride and nightmares of machine guns

Robbie Nolan: Age 1 baby

Dalton Joseph White: Age 12 Believer student

Jared William White: Age 10 Believer student

Audrey Ellen White: Age 7 Searcher student

Justin Louis White: Age 4 child

Monica Rose White: Age 2 child

Pam Rogers: Age 10 Believer student

Jane Rogers: Age 8 Believer Student

James Robert Paulson: Age 10 student hangs around Calvin when he can.

Samantha Mimm: Age 2 child

Douglas Morrison Jr.: Age 11 Believer Student

Thomas Morrison: Age 9 Believer Student

Howard Morrison: Age 7 Searcher Student

Peter Morrison: Age 4 child

Jason Morrison: Age 2 Named after Jason. Child.

Hope Morrison: Baby newborn cries to distract mercenaries and save James Paulson.

MISCELLANEOUS PERSONS MENTIONED

The Gov.: Age 37 Mercenary in the city where the plane lands who tries to collect taxes.

Lt: second in command of the Gov trying to collect taxes at the airport.

Ray (the Tinker) Desoto: Age-old, not stated. Believer Widower tinker fixes pots, Travels far and wide, and makes many friends, including the Fields. He avoids Mercenary if he can. Despite his gruff exterior, he has a kind, compassionate heart.

Margaret Desoto: Ray's deceased wife and the name of his horse.

Maria: Age 15, mind warped barmaid in village Dr. Carr is preaching in.

Mrs. Brown: Age 60 mind warped villager who put up Jason the last winter of his search. She was not a good cook.

Jed Linders: Age, 12 Non-Believer son of Inn keeper in the last town before the group from west, found. When the plane was seen, he attacked Calvin thinking he was mind warped, and he had revealed he was high tech; Calvin hit him with a shovel in the head.

CPSIA information can be obtained
at www.ICGtesting.com
Printed in the USA
BVHW030826021222
653294BV00014B/226